TYE WATKINS IN

A REASON TO KILL

GARY MCMILLAN

Cover concept and design by Michael McMillan

ISBN Number 978-0-9844730-9-0

This book is a work of fiction. People, events and situations are the product of the author's imagination. Any resemblance to actual persons, living or dead, or historical events is purely coincidental.

Published by Author's Discovery
Cooperation, Inc.

4608 Clover Ave

Odessa, Texas

432-553-2308

Printed in the United States of America

Books in the Tye Watkins Series

Border Trouble

The Crossing

Yancey

The Desperate Trail

Drums Along the Border

Back To the Rockies

Second Chance

Yahzie-Apache Warrior

Tye Watkins-U.S. Marshal

A Reason to Kill

Tye Watkins

After years of fighting Apaches and border bandits while scouting for the U.S Army Tye had decided to make a career change. With a wife and now two children to care for he took the offer presented to him to become a Deputy United States Marshal and track down thieves and killers. Even though this job was dangerous also, he knew it could not be as anything close to as bad as chasing the Apache-or so he thought.

In the first two months of his new job he had brought in or killed several thieves and murderers including the Frazier gang, the vicious killer, Bloody Jack Gillespie, and the murdering half-breed, Two Bears. But, when you have the reputation of being the best tracker in Texas, you are going to get the toughest jobs the State has to offer and there would be no easy assignments. This was the case for the last two years.

The Mills gang, led by brothers Willie and Lester, were reportedly headed in Tye's direction after, of all things, walking into a saloon in San Antonio and holding up the patrons that were there as well as taking about $4,000 from the saloon's safe. Five people died before the gang got out of town, none of which was any of the Mills gang.

The Mills brothers had been on the 'wanted list' of the state for several years. Somehow, they had eluded capture and had killed along the way a sheriff and two marshals that had tried to bring them in. They had sworn they would not be taken in to hang and any law dog who came after them was asking to meet his maker.

This is the challenge that Tye faced with friend, Deputy U.S. Marshal Sam Jenkins. Sam had proven more than once that he was a man to ride the river with. The two of them had teamed up several times since Tye became a marshal. Tracking down the Mills gang would prove to be one of the most dangerous assignments Tye had ever accepted, including his time fighting Apaches.

Chapter One

August 22, 1873

Willie Mills hesitated as he stepped thru the swinging half doors of the Alamo Saloon to let his eyes adjust from the bright sunlight to the dimness of the room. The first thing he saw was his younger brother standing at the far end of the bar. Walking to the near end of the bar he made eye contact with the other five members of his gang who were sitting at different tables. None made it known they were friendly with each other. Over the past two hours each man had come in alone so as not to draw attention. The boss was here now, and each knew things were fixing to get lively.

Willie Mills was quite a specimen of a man, standing well over six foot tall and weighing two hundred and thirty pounds-none of which was fat. He was broad through the shoulders and narrow at the hips with nothing but muscle in between. He wore a wide brimmed hat with a high crown that was dirty and sweat stained. Other than being bigger than most men he looked like the average cowboy until one took a closer look. His Colt was worn low on his right hip and the holster was tied to his leg. His face was covered in a heavy, black beard and his eyes were like two black pieces of coal under the bushy eyebrows. His nose was crooked from being broken several times and the top of his right ear was missing having been bitten off. These things occurring from his favorite pastime which was beating the hell out of men with his fist when he wasn't robbing and killing them. When he smiled, and this was seldom, yellow tobacco stained teeth shown between thin, cruel, thin lips. He was a far cry from being considered handsome by the ladies.

"Beer," he said as the bartender looked his way. He flipped two bits on the bar when the man set the mug in front of him.

"Passing through or looking to stay awhile?" The barkeep questioned in a friendly tone.

"Ain't none of your damn business barkeep," Willie replied not even bothering to look at the man. He turned around and leaned back on the bar, his elbows resting on the counter top with the beer in his left hand, and as was his habit, his right always empty and near his gun. He raised the mug to his lips and drank the warm beer as his eyes scanned the room. There were eleven men in the room besides his men and most looked to be working cowboys with the exception of two men who appeared to be merchants and a man who sat with his back toward him. The man with his back to him had a Colt on his hip and appeared to be tied down. None of the men apparently had given him a second look.

He sat the mug on the bar and in a loud voice said, "Excuse me gents, but can I have your attention for a moment." He waited for a couple seconds as men turned to look at him. “If you will look around you will see some of my friends have their guns trained on you so don’t do anything foolish.” He turned to the barkeeper. “My brother there,” he said nodding to the man holding a gun at the far end of the bar, will ask you just once to open the safe and remove the cash.” He looked back at the others. If you gents will be so kind as to skin yourselves of your guns we can commence with business.”

“W...We don’t have no s...safe,” the bartender said his speech showing his nervousness.

“Wrong answer,” Willie said as he turned back to the barkeep and lashed out with his pistol, the barrel catching the man across the mouth. The sound of broken bone and teeth could be heard by everyone and men winced at the sound. The man screamed and placed his left hand over his mouth, his right holding himself upright on the bar. Blood ran freely through his fingers and tears welled up in his eyes. “One more time barkeep,” Willie asked as the sound of his Colt being cocked rang loud in the quiet room. “Where’s the damn safe.”

A voice from behind him caused Willie to look over his shoulder. One of the two men who looked like merchants was speaking. "He can't open the safe even if he showed you where it was."

"Just who the hell are you?" Willie asked.

"Joe Barnes," the man answered. "I own this place. I'll show your man to the safe just don't shoot Jamie there," he said, nodding to the barkeep.

"That's fine," Willie said, "but I'll send you to hell without a second thought if you don't get your ass over here and get it opened and quick" The chair scraping on the floor as the man stood up broke the dead silence that had fallen on the room. As he stood up the man who had had his back to Willie stood up and the sound of Colt's being cocked came from the outlaws. The man turned slowly around to face Willie, the star on his vest gleaming under the lamps hanging from the ceiling. The man was careful not to let his hand get too close to the butt of his Colt.

The man smiled and chuckled, "I've heard of robbing banks, stagecoaches, trains, and even Wells Fargo offices, but I'll have to admit I've never heard of anyone robbing a saloon." His remark brought nervous laughter from some of the patrons. They promptly shut up as Willis walked up to the sheriff and without warning buried his big left fist in the man's belly. When the sheriff doubled over Willie hit him hard in the back of the head with the barrel of his Colt. The unconscious man hit the floor without uttering a sound.

"Don't have any use for lawmen," Willie said. One of the cowboys stepped toward Willie. Willie's Colt spewed hot lead and the heavy slug hit the cowboy square in the chest, the force of the bullet raising him off his feet and backwards hitting the wooden floor hard with his back. "Any of you other bastards feel like dying today?" No one moved or said anything.

"GOT IT," Lester Mills shouted from behind the bar holding up the money bag.

Willie nodded and turning back to the patrons pointed at a skinny man holding a gun. "My man there will pass in front of each of you with his hat in his hand. I expect each of you to empty what you have in your pockets and put it in the hat. I want to see your pockets inside out.

"And if'n we don't," a stocky cowboy said, there's more of us than you and we all have guns." Willie's Colt roared again and the man crumpled to the floor with his hands over the hole in his stomach trying to stem the flow of blood. The other men quickly emptied their pockets and put the contents in the hat, their eyes on their friend who lay moaning on the wooden floor, his life draining out of him.

"Anyone else have a leaky mouth?" Willie asked. No one said a word and the clinking of coins could be heard as they were dropped in the hat. "Didn't think so," the outlaw stated.

"Rufus," he said nodding to one of his men closest to the door. "Take a look outside to see what's going on. "Rufus backed to the door still holding his hog leg on the men in the saloon. Reaching the door he peeked over the bat winged doors.

"Crowds gathering," he said.

"Okay," Willie said. "Let's vamoose. As they moved toward the door the saloon owner reached under the bar and came up with a shotgun. Lester's bullet struck him in the throat just an instant before the barrel of the shotgun was level. The force of the bullet sent the man backwards and his finger tightened on the trigger. The buckshot went upwards and hit the chandelier holding the lamps. Oil and fire sprayed the patrons and the floor. The outlaws rushed outside and mounted their horses turning them around and taking off at a gallop. The outlaws in the back of the pack, Jarrod and Billy, turned and fired their pistols at the men coming out of the saloon knocking two of them down. Everyone else took cover and no more shots were fired as the men rode hell bent for leather out of town.

Chapter Two

One hundred and ten miles west of San Antonio lay the town of Brackett. Brackett was on the north side of the Old Mail Road which ran from San Antonio through Brackett, north up to El Paso and then west to San Diego. On the south side of the road directly opposite of Brackett was Fort Clark. The fort was established in 1852, but was abandoned during the Civil War and then re-garrisoned after the war in 1866. Several other forts were built in a line of defense against the Comanche, Apache, Kiowa and the Border bandits that had taken over the land while the army was away. In the years following the war, life along the Texas Mexico was precarious at best.

Tye sat at the table with his wife, Rebecca and Buff drinking coffee. Buff's real name was Shakespeare McDovitt, an old mountain man who had been Tye's pa's best friend while trapping beaver in the Rockies many years ago and he now lives with Tye and Rebecca. He's 74 years old, never married, and for the first time has a real home and around children. Tye and Rebecca had two small children, Ben and Nicole, who were still asleep.

Tye had been home for two weeks since his last assignment as a Deputy U.S. Marshal. He spread several wanted posters on the table which had come in last night on the coach from San Antonio. Rebecca picked one up that had a drawing of a very young man on it.

"This one is so young. He doesn't look to be a day over fifteen," she said. Tye took the poster from her and smiled as he read about the man.

"Kyle Lambert is the man's name and he's twenty years old. He's wanted for robbery and murder." He read a little more before speaking again. "Seems like he robbed his step daddy, killed him and then tied his mother to a chair. His ma was almost dead from lack of food and water before she was discovered by some neighbors. Sounds like a youngster that one would want to try and raise," he said shaking his head.

"Whut in tha world wud make a youngster want to do that?" Buff asked.

"I bet his stepfather was a brutal man and was extremely harsh on the young man and he just exploded one day after having enough abuse," Rebecca replied. Tye smiled because that was one of the things, among many, that he loved about his wife-her ability to find good in everything or anyone no matter what had happened or what that person had done. God knows she had somehow seen some good in him. When he met Rebecca he was a 'lost' man-both parent's dead and scouting for the army here at Clark. He had developed quite a reputation as a scout and Indian fighter who never lacked courage in a battle. After thinking back on it, hell, it wasn't so much courage as it was he just didn't care if he lived or died. He had no one to care for or care for him, nothing to live for. That all changed the minute he laid eyes on Rebecca.

He was protective of her to an extreme because he knew a lot of men didn't care much for him, friends of men who he had tracked down or killed over the years. He worried over her when he was gone because even living inside the fort's boundaries; civilians came and went every day. Buff living here helped alleviate some of his worry, but he knew men who would kill Buff or anyone else to get at Rebecca to extract some sort of revenge on Tye.

Footsteps on the porch caused all of their eyes to turn toward the door and Tye quickly stood and grabbed his Colt from its holster hanging on the peg by the door. He opened the door just as Sam Jenkins was about to knock. Sam was also a Deputy U.S. Marshal and he and Tye had been on several assignments together and had become pretty close friends.

Sam, seeing the Colt in Tye's hand threw up his hands. "I surrender," he said laughing.

"Sam," Tye uttered. "What in tarnation you doing here? I thought you were still laid up sick."

"I've sat on my behind for as long as I can stand it. I had to get up and move around and besides, I've got this," he said handing Tye an envelope which was addressed to both men. Sam had already opened and read it. He was quiet as Tye read it other than saying hello to Rebecca and Buff.

Having read the letter he laid it on the table. “Well, looks my next assignment has been decided for me,” as he picked up the wanted posters off the table, folded them and walked over and put them in one of his saddle bags. Rebecca took the letter from his hand and read it and sat down in a chair.

“These men sound so dangerous,” she said.

“That’s why Sam and me have to find them and bring them in before they kill someone else,” Tye replied looking down at her and placing his hand under her chin and lifting her face up. “It’s okay, honey. We’ve seen worse varmints before.”

It’s beyond me why some men do what they do,” Buff said.

Sam spoke up. “You have two kinds of men in Texas and I suspect everywhere else; those that are honest, God fearing family men who work honest jobs to raise their families and then those that are just too lazy to work and try and take what the honest men have. I suspect it will always be that way."

"I think you are right about that Sam," Tye said. "Besides," he chuckled, "those men keep me and Sam working so you," he pecked Rebecca on the cheek, "can have the things you deserve."

"Oh Tye, now don't you go using me as an excuse to do what you are doing," she said.

"I can always go back to chasing Apaches," Tye said.

Rebecca stood up and put her arms around him. "I just worry about you whether its Apaches or outlaws," she said burying her face against his chest.

"I promised you a long time ago that I would always come back to you-and I will."

"I'll see to it, you can count on that Mrs. Rebecca," Sam said. "I'll wait outside Tye while you get your things together and say your goodbyes." He stepped outside on the porch followed by Buff. This was the first time Sam since he helped Tye on Tye's first assignment over a year and a half ago that he had been alone with the old mountain man that he had heard so much about from Tye and others.

"We had some of those type of men back in the Rockies whilst Ben, that's Tye's pa, and me where trapping beaver," Buff said. "They weren't no law in the mountains so ifin' they got caught they were shot or hung on the spot and no questions were asked."

"I guess it was pretty tough in the mountains back then," Sam said.

"It took a special breed of men I guess," Buff answered. "At the time it didn't seem so special, but as I look back on it," he paused a few seconds his mind going back to those years, "it was. I mean you had temperatures that sometimes were thirty below, snow ten or twenty foot deep, you had grizzly bears that killed a great number of us, and then you had the Blackfoot, the Bloods and other tribes that hated us for coming into their land and killing the game. Very few of us were lucky enough to last mor'n four or five years before being killed or giving up and leaving to go back to civilization. Bridger, Ben, and me and few more lasted fifteen years or so. We were lucky."

"Or just damn tough," Sam noted.

"Tye's pa was the bravest, toughest man I ever saw," Buff said. "Tye is the spitting image of him. When I first came here to Clark and I saw him, I thought I was looking at Ben's ghost. It was plumb scary."

"How did you end up all the way down here from up in the mountains?"

"I was scouting for the army in Colorado and I heard stories from soldiers about this young man in Texas that was making quite a name for himself along the border of Mexico as a scout and Indian fighter. When I heard his name was Watkins and that his dad had been a mountain man, I just had to go and see if he was Ben's son. I knew Ben had settled in Texas and I received a letter from him telling me he had a son. That was a few years before I heard Ben had been killed. I started down many times to see Ben, but something always came up and then it was too late. I wasn't going to let that happen again so I came down to see Tye. I found a home for the first time in sixty or so years and have a family for the first time."

"I'm glad for you Buff," Sam said placing his hand on the old mountain mans shoulder. "You deserve it."

Tye came out the door after having said his goodbyes to little Ben and Nicole. Rebecca stood beside him and stood on her toes to kiss him on the cheek. "You be careful you big galoot."

"Always am," Tye said kissing her on the lips. "See you soon," he said as he and Sam headed to the stables.

Chapter Three

August 25th, 1874

The Mills gang sat on their mounts on the Old Mail Road five miles east of Uvalde which was forty-five miles east of Fort Clark. They had ridden hard from San Antonio stopping only long enough to rest the horses and get a few hours sleep.

Willie was doing the talking. "You can bet your last nickel that the law in Uvalde has been notified about our possibly heading their way," he said nodding to the telegraph lines that ran along the side of the road. "Just to be on the safe side of things I'll ride in alone and look over things. They are looking for several men so no one should suspect a single cowboy riding into town." He pointed to a stand of oak trees about a quarter mile north of the road. "We'll make camp there and ya'll can wait till I get back." He reined his mount off the road and headed toward the trees with the other following him without questioning his decision. The last gang member that questioned Willie was dead, drilled through the heart by a slug from the leaders Colt about three months ago. Since then his orders were followed without question by the others.

Two hours later found the outlaw sitting at table in the first saloon he came to in Uvalde. A man named Reading Black had a surveyor lay out the site for the town which would be named Uvalde. The original name given to the site by Mr. Black was Encino but was changed in 1855 to Uvalde. Nearby Fort Inge which was established in 1849 to protect the mail road that ran from San Antonio to El Paso. It was one of several forts built for that purpose including Fort Duncan, Camp Verde, Fort Clark and Fort Davis among others. The fort had recently been evacuated and the troops sent to Fort McKavett. The fort was now the home of a company of Texas Rangers.

Willie minded his own business and listened to the talk from the men at the two nearby tables while drinking his beer.

"I tell you Jasper, those killers are headed this way sure as not," one of the men said.

The one called Jasper replied. "George, you're always jumping the gun with your dad-blame assumptions. San Antonio is near a hundred miles from here. What makes you so sure they're headed this way? They might've headed north or south or doubled back and went around San Antonio towards Houston. Hell fire, there's a thousand ways they could've gone besides heading here."

"Where's the safest place for a man who's wanted by the law," George said. "I'll tell you-it's Mexico and straight west on the Mail Road is the quickest way to get there."

Well, maybe..."Jasper replied but was interrupted.

"Ain't no maybe about it, Jasper. Them there boys will be through here today or tomorrow. You'll see."

Willie turned in his chair and looked at the men. "Excuse me, but I couldn't help but overhear your conversation. Who are ya'll talking about coming here?"

"The Mills gang." George answered. "I'm sure you've heard of them. They kill men, women, children, and even dogs and cats if they are in the way."

"I'm new to these parts so I can't say I've heard of them. Women and children you say?"

"That the way the story about them goes so I hear," George said.

Willie was a little more than amused at the story especially about the children, dogs and cats. He stood up. "Guess I'd better go then," he said. I don't want to meet no baby killers."

"Whatcha name mister", Jasper asked since he knew just about everyone in town.

"Willie Mills Jasper, and If'n I was you or George there, I wouldn't stick my head out that door for a few minutes. Your leaky mouth talk about me killing babies and dogs and cats done soured my milk so this here baby killer just might blow your damn head plum off your stupid ass shoulders. *Comprende?"*

The two men just stared at Willie. Jasper's over sized adam 's apple in his skinny neck bobbed up and down a couple times like he was trying to swallow the words he had said earlier.

"Y...ye...yes sir...we won't,"George said.

"Good because if I kill children and dogs I sure as hell won't hesitate one second to kill the likes of either of you." He made a move like he was drawing his Colt and Jasper turned his chair over falling backwards hitting the floor hard. Willie laughed as he was walking out the door.

Arriving back at the camp Willie told them of the situation. "We can forget about going to Uvalde. The law has been notified about us and they are looking for us to ride in. We'll swing south of the town and get back on the Old Mail Road on the other side and keep heading west toward Mexico. I hear the pretty senoritas in the town of Piedras Negras love gringos, especially those with money to spend." They all had a good laugh and with a few hoots and hollers mounted their horses and followed Willie.

Tye and Sam rode into Uvalde about noon. Their first stop was the office of Sheriff Bill Wheeler. Entering the office they found Wheeler sitting behind his desk cleaning his fingernails with a folding knife. Looking up at the two men he laid the knife down and spoke.

"What can I do for you gents?"

Both men pulled their badges and showed them. "I'm Deputy Tye Watkins and this hombre with me is Deputy Sam Jenkins. You Sheriff Wheeler?"

"Bill Wheeler," the man said standing up and reaching across the desk shaking both men's hand. "You the Tye Watkins from Fort Clark?"

"Yes sir. I was a scout for them for two and half years or so before accepting the marshal job."

"Heard a lot about you. Why did you give up chasing Apaches?"

"I figured chasing outlaws was safer than Apaches. After my first few assignments I'm not so sure it is," Tye answered smiling.

"Damned if you're not probably right. This country is crawling with scalawags too lazy to work and eager to take what someone else has worked for." He leaned back in his chair and asked them to have a seat. "Now, what can I do for you?"

Sam answered. "We've word that a gang of outlaws led by Willie and Lester Mills were headed west from San Antonio and thought maybe you had seen them or any strangers in town.

The sheriff scooted his chair back and stood up. "Come with me," he said walking through a door that led to where the prisoners were kept in several cells. "I was out of town and didn't get back till about an hour and half ago. I found these two," nodding to a cell where two men lay on wooden beds with a thin straw filed mattress's, "drunk and falling all over people at Kelsey's saloon. I put them here to sober up."

Tye and Sam looked at each other and then at the sheriff. "What have they got to do with the Mills gang," Tye asked.

"Jasper," Wheeler said speaking to the men in the cell. The man mumbled something and raised himself up off the bed. "Jasper, come over here and be damn quick about it." To Tye's and Sam's amusement, the man stood shakily to his feet and fell back on the bed. The man in the other bed rose up and tried to focus his eyes on the men outside the jail. "George, you and Jasper need to tell these two U.S. Marshals what you told me a little while go as to why you were drunk." George seemed a little more sober than Jasper so he swung his feet off the bed and sat on the edge. "You gonna let us out Bill?"

"Just as soon as you and Jasper are sober enough to get your carcasses home. I already told your wives where you were at so they wouldn't worry none."

"Thanks sheriff." He looked at Tye and Sam and spoke. Jasper and me was in Kelsey's having a beer. This here stranger walked in and sat down at a table next to ours and was sipping his beer. We didn't pay him no never mind and went on talking about this gang of outlaws that was headed our way. It was supposedly the Mills gang and we were just talking about what we had heard about them killing men, women and children and even dogs. Anyway, whiles we were talking this gent asked us real polite like just who we were talking about. Old Jasper over there," he said nodding toward the bed, "well he likes to flap his lip so he just commenced to tell this man who the Mills gang was and what sorry men they were and they were supposed to be headed our way after robbing and killing some men in San Antonio." He wiped his lips with his sleeve. "I sure could use a drink Sheriff."

"Just finish your story and I'll get you one."

"Thanks . Anyway, like I was saying this here gent listened to what Jasper was saying then stood up and started to leave and we asked him his name.

He looked at us and smiled. "My name is Willie Mills and if I was you two I would not stick my head out that door for awhile cause Ifin' you do, this here baby killer just might blow your stupid heads off."

"What did this man look like George," Tye asked.

"Big, ugly, and had eyes almost black that could burn through a man. His nose was crooked and he had a beard."

"Had part of his ear missing too," Jasper said lying on his bunk and not even looking at the men. We thought he was going to shoot us right then and there. Scared me and George so bad we just plum got drunk."

"From the description we have that sounds like Willie alright," Sam said.

Tye nodded his agreement. "What did you do sheriff?"

"I have a deputy east of town that will ride back and tell me of any group of men coming this way. All the store owners here have seen their share of fights with outlaws and Indians and each of them have a gun belted on and ready for any trouble. They come here not all of them will leave." The sheriff led them back to the front office.

"Don't forget my drink Bill," George hollered as the door shut. The three men took their seats again.

"Don't think you will have to worry none about them coming here sheriff." Sam said. "Willie I bet came in alone just to see if the town knew of their heading this way."

"I'd bet my last dollar they will skirt town and keep heading west toward Mexico, Tye said while standing up. "Between here and México is Brackett and Fort Clark. The telegraph lines are not all the way there yet so they are not going to have any idea trouble is headed their way. Let's get going Sam." They headed to the door and stepping out, Tye looked back at the sheriff. "Thanks sheriff," and shut the door. He and Sam quickly mounted their horses and headed back the way they had come.

Chapter Four

August 26th, 1874

Willie and his men rode into Brackett shortly mid-afternoon the next day and headed to the first saloon they saw. Jim, standing behind the bar was the owner and he had seen his share of bad men before. From past experiences over the years he knew immediately these men were trouble and he moved down the bar to where his shotgun would be in easy reach. “What can I get you gents,” he said real friendly like as the men came up to the bar.

"Whiskey for starters one of the men said. As Jim poured the drinks he noticed the man who had done the talking was one ugly son-of-a-bitch, and bigger than his friend Tye Watkins, and not too many men were bigger than Tye. He went back to cleaning glasses, but kept his ears open.

"How long we staying in this one horse town Willie,"?

If looks could kill the look Willie gave Lester would have done the trick. "If you weren't my damn brother Lester, I'd shoot you dead for saying my name out loud," Willie whispered.

Lester knew he had screwed up. He whispered back at Willie. "Sorry about that. I wasn't thinking."

"That's why I run this rag tail bunch-I have to do all the thinking. Now don't say another word or I'll knock your damn teeth down your throat."

Willie looked at Jim and smiled. "How about another round barkeep?"

"Lookee yonder," Rufus Green the youngest of the bunch said looking out the window of the saloon. They all looked and saw what Rufus was talking about.

"Gawd Almighty," Lester said. "If that ain't the most beautiful damn woman I ever did see in my whole miserable born days." They all walked over to the window and door and looked out. Rebecca was walking down the street with Buff planning on going to the mercantile store. Mrs. O'Malley was watching her two children for a while.

Several obscene remarks were made about what they would like to do to her and Jim overheard and walked over to see what they were talking about. He was shocked to see Rebecca Watkins and Buff, and that she was the focus of their attention. He hurried back to the bar where his shotgun was and checked to make sure it was loaded. He leaned it against the bar within easy reach.

"You boys," he said loudly, "Need to come on back over here and have another beer or get on your horses and mosey on out of town.

"We ain't hurt'n nutin or no one barkeep so mind yur own damn business," Lester said.

Jim reached down and picked up the shotgun and laid it on the top of the bar with the barrel pointing in their general direction, his finger on the trigger. All he would have to do is lift the barrel up with his left hand and squeeze the trigger. Willie saw the danger in the situation immediately. He shrugged his shoulders and said, "Come on boys, let's belly up to the bar." He thought to himself though, *I'm gonna kill this damn barkeep before I leave and I'm sure gonna have some fun with that filly.*

"Just thought I would save you boys a lot of pain and suffering by suggesting ya'll mind your ways as far as that lady is concerned. She is the wife of Tye Watkins whom I'm sure ya'll have heard about if you have been in Texas long."

"Never heard of him," Willie said wiping the foam off his beard with his sleeve. "Who the hell is he?" Before Jim could speak Jarrod Coates spoke up. Jarrod was next to the oldest in the gang.

"He's bad news Boss," he said. "He's made a name for himself out here fighting Apaches and tracking down outlaws. Supposed to be meaner than an Apache too."

Jim took up the talk hoping to convince the men of what would happen if they messed with Rebecca. He thought stretching the truth a little would help. "The man's right. He about your size mister, nodding to Willie, and ain't ever, and I mean ever, lost a fist fight in his whole damn life. He was raised not far from here and his pappy was a famous mountain man who trapped with Jim Bridger and that fellow you seen walking with his wife while ago, Shakespeare McDovitt. His pappy taught him how to track, fight with his fist, wrestle, fight with knives and tomahawk, and he's better than any Apache at any one of them." He laughed, "Why last month a stranger came into town and confronted his wife on the streets and made some pretty nasty remarks to her in front of other people. That night they found him hanging upside down by his balls outside of town deader than a piece of wood and that feller had just talked to her. I'd hate to think what he would do if someone actually laid a hand on her."

"Sounds like somebody needs to bring this high and mighty bastard down a notch or two," Willie said.

"A lot of men have tried," Jim said smiling. "When he was with the rangers he tracked so many bandits down a bounty was put on his head. No one could collect it. He killed his first Apache when he was fourteen with a knife. He's been fighting them now for over fifteen years and has been on their most "wanted list" forever. He's still here and a hell of a lot of them aren't. Besides, Tye is so well liked by everyone around here if anything happened to Rebecca the whole damn country side would come down on whoever it was. They would not have a safe place to hide."

How come he didn't hang that feller by the neck," Lester asked.

Jim chuckled playing out the story as far as he could. "I guess because his throat was cut from ear to ear and Tye or whoever figured his head would come off he hung him by the neck. The way it was done put out a message that if you messed with Rebecca you were sure as hell gonna pay for it."

"Tell'um about the Mexican bandits who he brought in and wanted to get some information from them about their Alex Vasquez's whereabouts," one of the patrons at a nearby table said.

The outlaws who had turned to look at the man speaking turned back to Jim. "Three or so years ago the Alex Vasquez gang robbed an army payroll and killed the escort guarding it. I don't mean killed them in a fight but after capturing them, lined them up and shot them down. Tye tracked two of them down and brought them in after beating them half to death. They were put in the guardhouse at the fort across the road. They wouldn't talk so Tye encouraged them-Apache style. He pinned one the men's hand to a table with a Bowie-stuck it plum through the back of his hand and into the table. Every time the man hesitated giving an answer, Tye twisted the knife. He got what he wanted and pretty soon the whole damn gang was dead. I tell you boys, if you want to live to see your next birthday, don't mess with that gent."

"How about a bottle of your best whiskey," Willie said and as Jim turned to get it off the shelf Willie pulled his pistol. The men with him pulled theirs and covered the men at the table. When Jim turned back to them with the bottle he knew he had made a bad mistake. He was looking down the barrel of a forty-four caliber pistol. "Give me the money in the register," Willie said motioning with his gun. Jim opened the resister and took out the money and handed it to him.

"You men at the table empty your pockets and be damn quick about it," he added.

"Like hell I will," one of the men at the table shouted and turned the table over to use it as a shield and pulling his pistol at the same time. The table splintered as six pistols fired two to three shots apiece riddling the men at the table with bullets. Willie saw Jim reach for the shotgun and turned his Colt on him and squeezed the trigger. The forty-four caliber bullet caught Jim in the side of the head and brains and skull fragments exploded out the right side of his skull and spattered on the wall.

"Let's get the hell out of here," Lester almost choking on the smoke and acrid smell of gun powder shouted. They quickly mounted their horses and headed west racing out of town. Rebecca and Buff were crossing the street as the riders raced their horses in their haste to put distance between them and the town. Buff shoved Rebecca out of the way but he was struck by Willie's horse and knock head over heels into the side of a water trough.

Rebecca, shaken but not hurt ran to Buff who was not moving. “Please God,” she prayed. “Please not Buff- please. She sat down on the ground beside Buff and put his head in her lap, tears streaming down her face. People came running to her. “Please,” she cried. “Get a doctor.” Almost immediately soldiers who had came running from the fort at the sound of the shots were there led by Captain McClellan.

He turned to one of his men and ordered him to go get the post surgeon and then knelt down and placed a finger on the side of Buff’s neck looking for a pulse. He placed a hand on Rebecca’s shoulder. “He’s alive Rebecca. We don’t want to move him till the doc can check him for broke bones. He took off his tunic and covered the old mountain man with it.

“Th...Thank you Captain,” Rebecca sobbed. “God, I wish Tye was here,” she said laying her head on Buffs chest and sobbing uncontrollably. McClellan stood up as one of his men who had gone to the saloon came back.

“Four dead men there Captain- including the owner.”

"Jim is dead?"

"Yes sir. His head is almost clean blowed off."

McClellan stared off in the direction the killers had went. 'God help them when Tye see's all this," he mumbled to himself.

"You say something, Sir?

"No private. Just thinking out loud," McClellan answered.

"Here come sawbones," one of the soldiers said. The crowd that had gathered parted as the doc made his way to where Buff laid. He checked the pulse and then held a mirror over Buff's mouth-it barely fogged over.

"He's alive but barely," he said. "His pulse is weak and looks like his arm is broke." He picked up Rebecca's hand and helped her up. She leaned against McClellan. "I need to check him farther before we move him. You two," he said nodding to two privates that were stand close by, "Come here and help." The both knelt down beside Buff. "One of you hold his head still and the other take his feet and slowly, and I mean slowly straighten him out to where he is on his back." This accomplished, he made his examination.

He looked at Rebecca. "I want to be honest with you Rebecca. He's hurt and hurt pretty bad. I don't think anything else beside his arm is broken, but he has a bad bruise on the side of his head that I would guess from hitting the water trough. It's too early to tell if he is damaged internally. We'll just have to wait and see. He's a tough old codger and that will help." He walked over to the ambulance he had ridden in from the fort and removed a stretcher. "You men help me lift Buff onto the stretcher and get him to the post hospital. I'm going to see if I'm needed in the saloon." He placed his hand on Rebecca's shoulder and gave her a smile. "We'll do our best for him, Rebecca. Now you get in the ambulance and ride with him to the hospital."

Two hours later Tye and Sam rode into Brackett and immediately saw the crowd at his friends Jim's saloon. They tied their exhausted mounts to the hitching rail in front and went in to see what all the excitement was about. He was immediately mobbed by the townsfolk all speaking at the same time.

Tye held his hands up and hollered "Quiet down." He looked around as it become quiet and saw James Belcher, the blacksmith and a friend. "What's going on James?"

"Seven or eight men," he answered, "Rode in this afternoon and came into Jim's place

here. They ordered drinks and were real friendly like according to Bill Riley who was sitting at a table with Jim and Lee Waters and Les Whitaker. All was okay till one of the boys saw Rebecca crossing the street with Buff." Tye stiffened at the mention of Rebecca. "They were making some nasty comments about her when Jim set them straight about who she was and told them about you and there would be no place for them to hide if they touched her. They then set about robbing Jim and told us to empty our pockets. Well sir, you know Les, he wasn't going to let them take his money so he pulled his gun and all hell broke loose. Bill was wounded, shot twice, and Les, and the Waters brothers were killed right off. Jim made a move for his shotgun and they blew the side of his head off."

"Jim is dead,"? Tye questioned. James nodded.

"That ain't all Tye. As they rode out of town Rebecca and Buff were crossing the street. Buff got Rebecca out of the way but he was hit hard by one the horses and knocked head over heels into the water trough."

Tye gripped the edge of the bar so hard his knuckles were white. "And?"

"Don't know any more Tye. They took him to the fort's hospital. Rebecca rode in the army ambulance with him."

"let's go Sam," Tye said and hurried out the door and leading their mounts, walked across the road and Los Moras Creek into the fort heading straight for the hospital. Arriving there, they found several troopers there including Captain McClellan and Major Thurston.

Seeing Tye both officers hurried to him. "How's Buff," he asked shaking both men's hand.

"Glad you're here Tye," Thurston said. "He's not regained consciousnesses yet. He has a nasty bruise on the side of his head. His left arm was broken and he's bruised up some. Doc doesn't know about internal injuries yet."

Tye nodded. "Where's Rebecca?"

"She's in there with Buff. She hasn't left his side for a moment. The children are with the O'Malley's," McClellan replied.

Tye walked to the curtain was and pushed it aside. Rebecca jumped up from the chair and rushed into his arms and sobbed. "Tye...Tye. I'm so thankful you have gotten back. Buff," she sobbed even harder, "Buff could have gotten out of the way but he made sure I wasn't going to be hit and it was too late for him. God, Tye, he's hurt bad...so bad."

Tye pulled her to his chest. "It's going to be okay honey. You and I both know how tough that old man is." He looked down at his friend and a huge lump formed in his throat and he could not speak for a few seconds.

The post surgeon came around the bed to where Tye and Rebecca stood. He placed a hand on Tye's shoulder and looked down at the old mountain man. He's got a lot of injuries Tye but mostly superficial. The head injury is the worse unless he's tore up inside some which I won't know for awhile. With that head bruise he may be out for a few hours, a few days, or he may wake up in the next second. Brain injuries are still something the medical world is learning about. If it was any other man his age I would say the chances of recovery were slim, but this is one tough old son-of-a-bitch," he caught himself and asked Rebecca to excuse his language, "So I figure his chances are pretty good."

Rebecca sat back down in the chair and holding tightly to Tye's hand. Looking up at her man and tears still rolling down her cheeks asked. "Did you hear about Jim?"

Tye nodded and looked away. His good friend dead and Buff, who he loved dearly, almost dead. He looked up at the ceiling and silently spoke with God. *I haven't spoken to you in a while Lord and I'm truly sorry about that. Seems like the only time I do is when I'm in trouble or need some help like now. My friend Jim was a good man Lord. I didn't know his relationship with You, but I'm asking You to take him to Your bosom. I'm asking You, if it's in Your will, to heal old Buff there. He's been living by his lonesome for a lot of years, Lord, and now he's with people who love him- You know,family, so if it's in Your will, let him stay a little longer. He's a ornery old cuss, but I know he believes in You and I'm asking you to bring him back to those of us who love him. Thank You for listening.*

He knelt back down beside Rebecca. "I'm going to step outside the curtain and talk to Major Thurston and Captain McClellan, okay?" She nodded and released the grip she had on his hand.

Outside the curtain he walked to the three men, Sam, McClellan, and Thurston. "Those men have to be the Mills gang. We missed them in Uvalde and tracked them here. They killed my friend, Jim. They could have killed my wife, and they have hurt Buff, so bad," he paused to get the lump out of his throat. "He might not live. I figure they are headed to Mexico and are almost there. I'm going after them and I'm gonna kill every one of the bastards if it's the last thing I do."

"We can't cross into Mexico Tye," Sam said.

"I know I can't as a scout for the army or as a U.S. Marshal, but I can," he said handing the badge to Sam, "cross into it as an ordinary citizen. I am not going there to arrest them; I aim to kill them," he said in a tone that sent a chill up the men's spines. The two officers and Sam looked at a man they had not seen before; a man whose face had transformed from the warm, friendly face they were accustomed to, to a face that showed nothing but anger and hate.

"I can get some volunteers to go as civilians to help you," the major offered.

"Don't need any help Major."

"Damn Tye," McClellan said. "They are seven or eight hard cases you'll be after; men that won't hesitate for a second to kill you."

"Well I'm for one going with you," Sam said reaching to remove his badge."

Tye reached and grabbed his wrist. "I'm going alone Sam. You are not going to jeopardize your career helping me. If something happened to you," he said releasing his grip on Sam's wrist and placing it on his friends shoulder, "I would never forgive myself." He stepped back and looked at the three men-three friends. "This is something I have to do-for Jim and for what they did to Buff and damn near killing my wife. This bunch has killed a lot of people and I aim to make them pay in a way they understand, with this," he said patting his Colt with his hand. He turned and went back where Rebecca and Buff were.

^^

"I've known Tye a long time," Thurston said. "I've never saw him like that before."

"Me neither," McClellan said, "But I would not want to be in their boots when he catches up with them."

"Are you two crazy," Sam stated. "He's going after eight killers, men who have no qualms about killing. Do you think he has a snow ball chance in hell of pulling this crazy stunt off."

Both officers smiled and then Thurston said. "Sam, if you knew the man like we do, you'd feel sorry for those men. He'll find them... and he will kill them and that's something you can bet on. Hell man, he's taken on the whole damn Apache Nation for the last fifteen years and he's still here."

^^

"That may be true from what I've seen the last couple years, but still I think it's a long shot. He don't know it but I'm gonna be trailing him and watch his back. I know he don't want to take that pack horse into Mexico because even I know why that's not a good idea."

"Why's that if you don't mind explaining it to me," McClellan asked?

"There's a lot of poor people in Mexico and a lot of bandits. They may not pay any attention to a man on a horse but a man with a pack horse is telling everyone who sees him he's got some stuff, maybe not money, but things that are valuable."

McClellan nodded. "That makes sense."

"He thinks he's gonna leave the pack animal with me at the river so if you could major, have a man following us and after Tye leaves me, he can bring the horse back to you leaving me free to follow Tye."

Thurston rubbed his chin while thinking about it and then nodded. "We'll do it Sam, but let me give you a piece of advice as far as following Tye. Stay way back because I've seen him out of the clear blue sky and with no reason feel someone following him. He's one in a million and something special and we need him out here-alive." He shook Sam's hand and added. "Take what you need from the supplies when Tye leaves you at the border and then leave the horse tied to a bush. My man will be along after you leave to pick him up. You take care, Sam."

"I will major and oh yeah, I almost forgot. I'll leave my badge with the pack horse so tell your man to give it to you." Thurston nodded.

Chapter Five

August 27, 1874

Tye had left Fort Clark early the next morning. After explaining to Rebecca what he had to do he was surprised that she put up no argument. She was angry at what these men had done and if it had been possible she would have went with him and help kill them herself. Buff was still hanging on and had not regained consciousness when he left. He prayed that he would find him up and well when he returned. Thurston had made sure he had plenty of supplies and furnished him with a pack horse to carry them. Sam rode beside him to the Rio Grande but would not go into Mexico with him. At least that's what Tye thought.

~~

Now in Mexico, Willie had the men make camp just a few yards from the Rio Grande River. He felt safe now knowing the law would not cross the river into Mexico and the Mexican Federales had no reason to want him. He lay on his blanket with his saddle as a pillow and thought about his and Lester's life and how it could have been different. He thought of his mother and how loving she had been and then anger welled up inside of him as he thought of his father, and how he had been

He was born in southern Arkansas forty-two years earlier and had never had an easy life. His father was a brutal man who beat him and Lester unmercifully if they did not do exactly as he said. He was a heavy drinker and when he was drunk he would beat up on their mother. Their father up and left him, his brother, and his mother when Willie was ten years old. He had to go to work to keep his brother and mother in food. His mother took sick two years later and died of pneumonia leaving him and his brother alone in the world. They took to odd jobs from shoveling horse manure to swamping saloons to have enough money to buy something to eat.

They begin stealing things from the mercantile stores; a gun here and a coat there and selling them to supplement their meager earning from the other jobs they held. The second time they were caught, he was seventeen, and stood before the judge who sentenced them to prison for one year to teach them a lesson. This lesson backfired and many people paid dearly for it. Prison only hardened the young boys into bitter young men and when they were released the first thing they did was go back home and shoot the judge who had sentenced them. The second man they killed was six months later after tracking him down-their father.

On the run from the law in Arkansas they rode into the big state of Texas only to fall in with three other men who were young, but still older than either Willie or Lester. One robbery led to another with a killing throwed in for good measure ever now and then and soon every lawman in the State of Texas was looking for them. Over the years men in their gang were caught, some left of their qwn accord, and some were killed. The men with him now had been with him and Lester for quite awhile except for the two youngsters, Ben and Rufus. They were lifelong friends whose past had been much like Willie's and Lester's. Willie found them in a jail in a one horse town outside of Fort Worth six months ago. He needed men so he walked into the jail, convinced the sheriff he was one of the mens uncle and would like to talk to them. When the sheriff took his gun and turned to open the door leading to the cells Willie stuck a knife in his back and picked up the keys from the dead man's hand. He walked into the back where the cells were and asked the boys if they wanted out. They thought he was kidding till they spotted the sheriff lying on the floor. They were grateful and had been riding with Willie since. Now, they were hiding in Mexico with Willie.

"Hell of a life," he mumbled under his breath.

Lester looked over at him. "You say something?"

"Naw," Willie answered. "Just thinking out loud. You men get a little rest. We'll be moving out in a couple hours or so."

~~

Late afternoon shadows found Tye and Sam five miles from the Rio Grande. It would be dark by the time they reached the river so Tye thought it best they go ahead and make camp and he would cross into Mexico in the morning. Rocks were piled in a circle and a small fire was going before long, the flames shielded from prying eyes by the rocks. Water was put on to boil for coffee and bacon was put in the frying pan. Tye figured this would be his last hot meal for he didn't know how long so he was going to enjoy this one. He also was going to enjoy conversing with Sam because his camps would be lonesome for awhile.

Tye dropped the coffee grains in the boiling water and set the pot on the rocks. He dropped in a little cold water to settle the grounds and poured Sam and himself a cup. Each of them put some of the sizzling bacon in their plates and took biscuits and dipped them in the hot grease. Hot bacon with biscuits dipped in bacon grease along with steaming coffee was a feast for them.

"Don't guess you brought any of them cakes from the bakery?" Sam mumbled. His words were hard for Tye to understand with Sam's mouth full of biscuit.

"Nope, I didn't," Tye answered. "Figured you would be back at the fort tomorrow and getting all you want. As for me, never did much go for the cakes, but any kind of fruit pie is a whole different story," he said laughing. They ate in silence for a few minutes before Sam asked.

"What's your plan Tye? I mean they are seven or eight men you are after and from what I've seen and heard of them doing, every damn one of them is a half bubble off plumb, especially Willie and Lester. I figure men like that are about the most dangerous men you can chase."

"Don't reckon I know for sure till I find them and see what the situation is. You're right about them being about half crazy Sam, but my experience has always shown me that the outlaw ain't usually the brightest man on earth. I'll figure something out when I find them. They will probably be feeling pretty safe over in Mexico and sure won't be expecting anyone from Texas following them. That fact will work to my advantage plus they don't even know who I am or what I look like."

"They will soon enough and then they will be looking for you."

"I might have whittled their number down some by the time they know who I am," Tye replied. "I've never shot a man who wasn't facing me or trying to kill me. I may make an exception in this case."

"You mean to ambush them Apache style."

"That's what I'm thinking. Hit and run, kill one or two at a time and let the remaining polecats think about things they have done and who it is killing them. I hope to save Willie and Lester for last and then let them know who it is that's killed their friends and who is fixing to kill them."

"Sounds good Tye, but you know the type they are and they ain't going be that easy to kill after the first attack."

"Yeah, I thought about that. I'll just play it by ear after the first encounter." Tye emptied his cup on the ground and lay back on his blanket. "Let's get some shut eye."

~~

Back at the fort Rebecca was preparing to get Ben and Nicole settled in bed. It had been a long day with her sitting with Buff, holding his hand and talking to him even though he probably didn't know it and she was exhausted. The strain of possibly losing Buff and worrying about Tye was stretching her to the limit. She just sat down in the chair with a glass of tea when there was a knock on the door and a voice she recognized as Mrs. O'Malley was hollering at her.

"Rebecca...Rebecca come quick to the hospital. Old sawbones wants to see you right away." Rebecca ran to the door.

"What's going on?" she inquired.

"Don't know honey. Private Gail came to my house and just said to get you there pronto. He said he knew I would watch the young'uns for you."

"Thank you. I just laid the children down so they shouldn't be a problem." She threw a shawl around her shoulders and rushed out the door to find Senior Master Sergeant O'Malley waiting for her. He took her hand and they walked as fast s they could to the hospital.

Entering the hospital they went straight to where Buff was and drew back the curtain. To her surprise Buff was propped up on some pillow swallowing some broth that the doc was feeding him.

"Buff...Buff," she cried. "Buff you're okay," she said rushing to him with tears streaming dsown her face. She took his hand and held it to her cheek and wept openly.

"Now...now Rebecca," he said, "Everything is okay. No need to make a fuss over an old geezer like me." She put her head on her shoulder and he hugged her with his one good arm as a tear rolled down his cheek. He patted her on her back. "Everything is fine," he choked out. "Doc says I'll be as good as new in a few days."

Rebecca pulled back and looked at the old mountain man thru eyes full of tears. She leaned forward and kissed him on the forehead and then on the cheek. "I love you so much you old geezer," she said trying her best to laugh. " I've been so worried about you."

A lump was in Buff's throat and he had to clear it before he could speak. "Ain't nobody ever cared enough for me to act like this," he mumbled. "I tell you Rebecca, it's a damn good feeling and I'll tell you something else...something I ain't ever said before; you and Tye just don't know how I feel toward ya'll. I love you two like'n you were my own two kids and your two kids...my Gawd I worship the ground they walk on."

"We know that Buff-we're family."

Buff looked behind Rebecca. "Hey there sergeant."

O'Malley stepped to the bed and shook Buff's hand. "Great to see you back in the land of the living old timer."

"Where's Tye?"

Rebecca picked up his hand and held it. "Tye was really upset about what those men did Buff. They killed Jim at the saloon and three other men. Tye didn't know if you were going to live or die." She started crying again. "He...he turned his badge in and is headed to Mexico to find them."

"Jim...Jim is dead?"Buff said more of a question than a statement. Rebecca nodded.

"He'll find them and bring them back to pay for killing Jim," Buff added.

Rebecca shook her head. "He's not bringing them back. He...he's going to kill them. He was very upset Buff. I've never seen him so mad. I just pray that his anger doesn't get him hurt or killed."

Buff closed his eyes and laid his head back on the pillow. "Don't you worry your purty head none about Tye. When it's fighting time he's the coolest, most level headed man I ever saw besides his pa. He'll be fine Rebecca. Now then, you get on home and take care of my grandkids and I'll see you in the morning."

Rebecca nodded her head and gave Buff a big hug and a kiss on the cheek. "We are so thankful you are going to be okay. I'll see you in the morning." She placed a finger on her lips and then touched Buff's forehead with it. "Nite Buff."

Buff finished the last of the broth and the doctor removed the pillows he was propped up on so he could lie back flat on the bed with only one pillow under his head. After the doc left he lay thinking about what Rebecca said about Tye turning in his badge he had been so proud of and now on a trail of vengeance. He had known a man in Colorado who was tracking down the men who killed his wife and had caught and killed two of the four before he made a mistake and it cost him his life. The mistake he made was a stupid one and if he hadn't been so filled to the brim with hate and not thinking straight he would never had made it. He knew Tye and his temper but he also knew that he was level headed enough to think like a fox and would never make a careless mistake. With that thought he drifted off to sleep.

~~

"What you think, Jose?" Miguel asked his friend.

Jose looked at the two tables where the Americans sat drinking whiskey. "I think they are bad men and probably on the run from the law in Texas."

"Me too I think. I think with too much whiskey there be big trouble this night."

The outlaws found this little village by accident. They still did not know the name of it. Willie, sitting at the table with his brother, Brad Silver and Jarrod Cates looked the place over. Six Mexicans sat at two other tables and two stood at the bar. None seemed to be paying much attention to his bunch. Two young senorita's sat at another table by themselves. He turned to the table beside him where the rest of his gang sat, Billy Grey, James Herring, Rufus Green, and Ben Tyler. "You boys watch your manners tonight. I don't want any problems that might get the locals riled and draw attention to us. Understood?" Each man nodded.

One of the youngsters, Ben Tyler, spoke up. "What about the girls. Can we have a little fun with them?"

"Go ahead," Willie said. "No rough stuff and keep it quiet."

"That may be hard for the girl to do that's with me when I get started." Rufus chuckled. The others including Willie laughed.

"Just don't cause no problems," Willie said.

Ben and Rufus stood up and taking their drinks walked over to the table where the girls were and sit down. Willie watched them closely for any signs of trouble. Pretty soon though, the girls were laughing along with his two men so he quit worrying about them.

An hour later while Rufus and Billy were up stairs with the girls, trouble walked in. Three Mexicans that Willie figured to be banditos came in and stood at the bar. One was a huge man, probably six three or four inches tall and thick through the shoulders. He spoke to the man behind the bar and willie saw the big man look up the stairs. Willie whispered to the men at his table, "Trouble is here. Be ready." Each man shifted his body so that his gun was handy if needed.

The big Mexican glanced around the room, his eyes settling on the two tables where the gringos sat. He said something to his compadres and they looked also. Cole dropped his right hand off the table and onto his thigh and then with a slight movement that went unnoticed by the Mexicans pulled his Colt and held it in his lap. Cole looked at the other patrons of the bar and saw them getting up and leaving one or two at a time. They knew trouble was coming he figured and didn't want to get caught in a crossfire.

Chapter Six

Cole glanced at the stairs and saw the girl on Billy's arm eyes go wide when she saw the big Mexican. She jerked her arm from Billy's just as the big man shouted something in Spanish and went for his gun. Cole pulled the trigger on his Colt that he had under the table and the bullet caught the man in the knee. The two men with the big Mexican were startled at the sound of the gun from their right, but only for a second and then went for their weapons also. A hail of bullets from Cole, Leslie, Jarrod, and Brad cut the three men down as Billy and Rufus stood on the stairs wondering what the hell was going on.

The three men lay in a pool of blood each with at least two holes in them. There was no sound in the room as the smoke cleared and everyone could see. The acrid smell of gunpowder was thick as Cole and his men quickly reloaded.

"What the hell was that all about," Billy asked?

"Apparently the big Mexican was sweet on the girl you just poked," Cole said. The bartender was coming to the table where Cole sat.

"Senor," he said. "It is best you leave quickly."

"Why? He drew his gun first and we were just protecting ourselves," Cole replied.

"Makes no difference Senor," the man said. "That man," he said pointing to the big Mexican, was Jose Mendoza, a very bad hombre, but was nothing compared to his brother Louis. They have many men and will be looking for those that killed his brother."

Cole slammed his mug down on the table spilling most of its contents and glared at Billy and Rufus. "I hope you two peckerwoods had a good time with those gals because it looks like we'll be moving on and I'll make sure it will be your last poke for awhile." He stood up quickly. Let's get the hell outa here," and then looking toward Billy and Rufus added in a disgusted voice, "It would have been better for us to just have let them gun you down." Billy and Rufus swallowed the lump in their throats both knowing they could be dead right now and sure as hell better watch what they say and do for awhile. Cole was a dangerous man, but when he was mad, no telling what he would do. They mounted their horses without another word said and rode out of town with Billy and Rufus staying at the rear of the group as far away from Cole as they could get.

~~

Tye had ridden Sandy hard and when he rode into the little village it was only a couple hours after the outlaws had left. He knew Sandy was pretty well used up and needed some time to recuperate so he was hoping to be able to let him. He stopped in front of the cantina and let the big horse drink his fill from the trough before tying him to the hitching rail. Walking through the doors he noticed two young boys scrubbing the floor, cleaning up what looked like blood. Strolling over to the bar he looked at the man behind the counter.

"Speak English?" he asked.

"Si, Senor. A little." Tye looked back at the two boys scrubbing the floor.

"What happened? That looks like blood they are cleaning up."

"Si, Senor," the man said nodding. "It is blood. Three Mexican banditos were shot by some gringos." The word gringos got Tye's attention.

"When did this happen?"

"A short time ago, maybe two hours."

"Was there seven or eight gringos?"

The bartender thought a minute. "There were eight senor." He poured Tye a beer. "I think there will be much trouble now."

Tye took his finger and wiped the foam off the beer and took a swallow of the warm beer that tasted worse than he figured horse piss however bad that was. "Why trouble?"

One of the men killed was the brother of Louis Mendoza, the leader of a very bad bunch of banditos. They will be following them and they will kill the gringos.

Tye understood the fix he was in now. He would be following Cole and his bunch as would the Mexicans and who would be in between-Tye. "Damn", he mumbled under his breath. "How long you think before this here Mendoza and his bunch shows up?"

The bartender shrugged his shoulders. "Who can tell? I do not know where he is, but only that he will be here quickly when he hears what happened." He had not gotten the words out of his mouth when the sound of many horses could be heard outside. The bartender and Tye both looked at towards the door. "That is either Louis or the soldiers," he said. "Either is trouble." Tye took his beer and walked to a table and sat down, his back to the wall just as the bat winged doors flew open and four tough looking men walked in. Three of the men spread out against the wall as the fourth walked to the bar where the bartender was. Tye figured that was Louis. The man pushed his sombrero off his head and it lay on his back held by a leather strap around the man's throat. He had a set of bandoliers full of shells across his chest, a Colt on his right hip and a knife on his left. *A very dangerous looking man* Tye thought. Tye studied the man's face. He had a full beard that was in need of a trim. He had thick, bushy eyebrows and a set of the blackest eyes he had ever saw on a man other than an Apache. He looked like he could use a bath also as his clothes were filthy and he bet the man smelled to high heaven.

In a voice loud enough for everyone to hear he said, "I am Louis Mendoza and I am looking for the killers of my brother." His eyes scanned the room and settled on Tye. "I hear he was shot down like a dog by gringos," he said walking toward Tye.

Tye, his left hand wrapped around the mug of horse piss and holding his Colt in his right under the table said nothing. To everyone it appeared he was relaxed and just enjoying his beer. Louis stopped two steps from the table.

"What about you gringo?'" he asked in a loud voice. "You shoot my brother?"

Tye looked at him and answered with a smile. "Can't say I did. I just got here a few minutes ago, but if your brother was a loud, pompous ass as yourself. I might have."

Taken back by the remark the outlaw stuck a thumb to his chest. "Do you know who I am?"

Tye took a sip of beer. "Heard you say your name was Louis Mendoza."

"That name does not mean anything to you?"

Tye shrugged. "Nope. Should it?"

Something about this man bothered Louis. Something told him this was a dangerous man and also told him he was not the type to shoot a man down like he heard his brother had been. He looked over his shoulder at the bartender. "Bring me a beer and a fresh one for my friend." He looked at Tye. "May I sit?" he asked placing a hand on a chair opposite of Tye. For the first time he noticed Tye did not move his right hand.

Tye nodded and the big Mexican sat down just as the two beers arrived. "Gracias," he said.

"I would feel much better, Senor, if you would put your gun back in its holster and not pointing at my belly," he said smiling.

Tye smiled and said. "I will when your men there either sit at a table or go outside. Louis looked the men against the wall and then at Tye and then motioned to the men to leave.

"Senor, you are not a trusting man," he said holding his hands out, palms up. "I am an honorable man."

Yeah right, Tye thought. *And I might get elected President of the United States.* "I didn't get to be this old my not being careful Mendoza. Tye lifted his right hand holding the Colt and placed the gun of the table, the barrel conspicuously pointing toward his guest, his hand resting a couple inches from it.

Mendoza took a sip of beer and looked like he wanted to spit it out. Tye chuckled. "Taste like horse piss doesn't it?"

Louis sat the mug down. "Horse piss would be better." He leaned back in his chair. "Why are you here gringo? This part of Mexico is a dangerous place for a man such as you, a gringo."

"Looking for someone."

"A Mexican?"

"Nope. Eight Americano."

"Why you looking for them?"

"Look Louis. I don't have to explain shit to you as to why I do anything," Tye said sternly, "but since you asked I'll tell you. I'm gonna kill every damn one of them."

Taken back by this statement Louis again gestured with his hands. "You are only one man Senor and as you say, they are eight."

"The number makes no difference Mendoza. I'm gonna kill them and anyone who gets in my way. "Tye hoped this false show of brashness might convince the outlaw to not bother with him and that they were after the same thing.

"Why are you so set on killing these men?"

"They shot down a friend of mine in Texas and hurt another so bad he might be dead by now." This though of Buff being possibly dead brought a sudden lump to his throat.

"You would do this for a friend?"

"I set a lot of stock in a man who is a friend and if you hurt him, I will hurt you." He then added. "I believe in what the Good Book says somewhere in it; an eye for an eye."

Louis liked this gringo. He was a lot like him in some ways. "Why don't you ride with us and when we catch them you can have your fun with what's left over."

"How many men do you have riding with you?"

"Eleven now, but I can get more if needed."

"I think I will ride alone," Tye said as he stood up from the table.

"As you wish hombre. I think maybe you," he paused and rubbed his chin, "what is it you Americans say." He snapped his fingers and pointed at Tye. "You may have bitten off more than you can chew." He laughed and reached across the table and shook Tye's hand. "Good luck amigo," he said.

Tye nodded and waited till Louis stood up and walked ahead of him to the door not wanting to turn his back on this two-faced outlaw. *Men like him are more dangerous than the Apache,* Tye thought. *Shake your hand, pat you on the back and then shoot you as soon as your head is turned.* Tye stood in front of the cantina while Louis and his men mounted their horses. Louis tipped his sombrero to Tye. "We will meet again my friend," he said waving as he reined his horse around and headed out of the village.

I don't doubt that for a second, Tye thought as he walked to the hitching rail, unwrapped Sandy's reins and mounted. He nudged Sandy into a trot and followed the outlaws. He leaned forward in the saddle and patted Sandy on the neck after slowing him to a walk. "This little job just got a hell of a lot more complicated Sandy-a hell of a lot more.

A quarter of a mile behind Tye Sam was breathing easier. He was worried while Tye was in the village because he didn't know what was going on. He become really concerned when he saw the group of men ride in he figured was banditos and was elated when he saw Tye and them come out of the cantina. He couldn't figure out what was going on, but it appeared Tye and the one who appeared to be the leader were on speaking terms. He now watched Tye and Sandy through the binoculars Thurston had sent along with him. He was surprised when Tye stopped Sandy and reined the horse around to look at his back trail. It was too late for him to move into the brush so he just sat there waiting to see what Tye would do and cussing himself remembering what Thurston had said about Tye having an extra sense that told him things like when someone was following him or trouble was coming or it was going to rain tomorrow and any of a thousand other things that a normal man would not know.

Sam knew one thing for certain, he, Tye, those men in front of Tye and the outlaws they were all following were all going to end up in a one place sooner or later and all hell was going to break loose.

Chapter Seven

August 29th, 1874

Tye, sitting on a boulder in the shade of a cliff and letting Sandy have a break was chewing over the way things were and trying to sort things out. From reading the tracks he was staying a few minutes behind Mendoza and probably no more than two or so behind Willie and his bunch. Despite the situation Tye had to chuckle. *I wonder if any lawman has been in this situation; following a gang of cutthroats who are following another gang of even worse cutthroats.* He checked his Colt and placed a forty-four cartridge in the chamber under the hammer that he normally left empty like most men did. A lot of men had had been wounded by the hammer being accidently drawn back by a limb while riding thru brush and released on a loaded chamber. He also checked his Henry to make sure it was fully loaded and ready for action.

He looked across the land before him and thought again how much it looked like Texas and he loved it even though to most it was an ugly, barren land good for nothing except the coyotes, rattlesnakes, and Apaches. There were however, a great number of folks who saw it his way and were trying to make a go of it out here. These people were the reason he was doing what he does best-tracking down outlaws and occasionally, Apaches.

He knew himself and others like him were slowly bringing some law and order to this part of Texas. Before, a man had to handle a wrong done to him by another with his fist or a gun. That was the only law out here-the law of Samuel Colt who made all men regardless of size, equal. In the cities, if a man was done wrong by someone you had the law to handle it. Out here, a man had to handle his own problems and if he didn't, lost any respect he had by other men. Always fight your own battles and never back down even if you know you are going to get your butt kicked was what youngsters was raised to believe, so that was the way it was. For the most part it was a good thing, but more and more disputes ended up in a gun fight instead of with his fist.

He never had any schooling, but his ma had made sure he learned to read, write and do numbers. She also made sure he knew what the Bible had to say about things like; how to treat people; to have respect for parents and elders; how it was wrong to kill another human; and to respect others property. He knew most of these lessons from his ma had shaped the way he always treated people. The one about killing another human he had trouble with until his pa explained it. "Son," he said. "I know what the Good Book says about killing another man, but it also says an eye for an eye and a tooth for a tooth. I take that to mean if a man kills another man then he should expect the same fate. There are just some men that don't deserve to be on this earth because of what they do to their fellow man. I sure don't think the Good Lord would blame a man for killing someone who was trying to kill him or his loved ones. I don't hold what a ranger captain once said about some bad men they were chasing; 'kill'um all and let God sort them out.' But as I reflect back and think about some of the bad men I have known, that captain wasn't so far off track with what he said.

Tye looked up at the sky. "Pa," he said, "I've tried to live a good life like you and ma taught me, but you were right, there's just some men God put here for some reason that just don't deserve to be among the good folks." He brought his eyes down and looked at the countryside. "I wish you and ma were still here. Ya'll would love this country more than ever since lots of people were living here now. You wouldn't have to travel all day to find a neighbor like you did back then. Most of all," he said, his throat tightening up, "I wish you were both here to see my family and to spoil your grandkids. You'd be proud of old friend Buff pa. He's taking to being a grandpa like a duck to water. I have a notion you have gotten to know the Man upstairs so you might bend his ear some and ask him to look at Buff and let him have more time on this earth with us." The thought of Buff lying in the hospital hurt so bad that he might not live brought tears to his eyes and he wiped them with the sleeve of his cotton shirt. He walked over to Sandy and stepped into the saddle. “Let’s go boy. We’ve got some bad varmits to catch.”

~~

Several miles to the east Willie held up his hand signaling his bunch to rein in. He had spotted some willows off to his left and figured there was water there. He turned in the saddle and spoke to his most trusted man, Brad Silver. “We’re going to give the horses a rest over there in those willows and oaks. I figure there’s water there so after you water your horse go back a ways and see if anyone is following.” Brad nodded and all headed to the willows.

After Brad left to check their back trail Willie had the two youngest members, Rufus and Ben, gather up some dry wood and start a small fire to make some coffee. “Make damn sure it’s dry. I don’t want no green wood making a lot of smoke,” he said after seeing Rufus pick up some limbs that still had green leaves on them.” *I swear,* he thought to himself, *if those two’s brains were dynamite they couldn’t blow the snot out of their noses.* A few minutes later a fire was going and water boiling. Billy dropped in some coffee grounds and let the water boil for a couple minutes then set the pot on a rock and poured in a little cold water to settle the grounds. A minute later the men were squatting around the fire with their tin cups sipping the hot liquid.

"Do you think we are being followed," Ben asked Willie.

Willie looked at the youngster and said in a disgusted voice. "No one would be if you and Rufus had kept your damn peckers in your pants. To answer your question, hell yes that man's brother is following us. Wouldn't you if some peckerwood shot your brother. If I had any sense I'd shoot you both myself and leave your sorry asses hanging from a tree with a note stuck on your shirt to Mendoza or whatever the Mex's name is saying these are the two that killed your brother."

Rufus chuckled. "Yu wundn't do that wud yu Willie?"

"You Gawddamn right I would in a heartbeat if'n I thought it would do any good, but I figure that son-of-a-bitch is so pissed off he won't just be satisfied with you two piss ants."

"Brad's coming back," Jason said standing and looking at their back trail.

All the men stood up as Brad rode up and quickly dismounted. "Didn't have to go far boss," he said slightly out of breath. "A dozen or so riders are coming behind us. They look like a bunch of Mex and they are definitely following our tracks.

"How much time do we have," Willie asked.

"Maybe twenty minutes behind us. They're pushing pretty hard."

"Damn," Willie cursed. He looked at the two young men, Rufus and Ben, and if looks could kill... . He then looked at the surrounding countryside. He could see no place they could hole up and defend themselves. "Give your horses another drink and let's light a shuck outa here. If those tamale eating hombres are pushing their horses as hard as Brad says they just might have to hole up here for awhile and give them a good blow. That might give us enough time to put a little more distance between us and them and maybe find a place to give them a little surprise."

~~

Tye, holding Sandy to a trot, was having no trouble following the trail of so many horses. He could go much faster with the trail as plain as it was, but he was staying back not wanting to accidently stumble on Mendoza and his bunch. The second meeting might not be as cordial as the first. Mood swings among men like that could change in an instant and he didn't want any part of that bunch anyway. He was just following to pick up whatever was left of the Mills bunch if the two groups met which he was sure they would. From the looks of the men he saw back in the village he figured they might not be anything left for him to clean up. He hadn't met Willie but he knew his and Mendoza's type-both meaner than a she bear with a sore teat and totally unpredictable.

A half mile behind Tye Sam was on a knoll looking at Tye with his telescope. Like Tye, he knew sooner or later the two gangs of outlaws were going to meet up and he figured Tye would be somehow in the middle of it. He just had to stay a safe distance behind Tye, but not so far as to not be able to offer help in a couple minutes. He decided to close the gap some and just be damn careful his old pard didn't see him following.

Thirty minutes later Sam rounded a bend in the trail and pulled up suddenly. Sitting on his horse in the middle of the trail was Tye with a look on his face that would pucker a hog's butt. "What do you think you are doing Sam,"? Tye questioned in a not to civil to tone.

Sam, getting over the shock of meeting his friend answered. "Just taking a few days off and seeing what Mexico's like."

"And you just happened to be on the same trail as me?""Hell fire, Tye. What in

thunderation are friends for if they don't look out for each other."

"Dad-blame it, I told you I wanted to do this myself and didn't want anyone else

helping that might get hurt or killed."

"Well, I'm here Gol-Darn it and I ain't going back so quick your bellyaching and

let's get on with it."

Tye sat there looking at his friend and the anger left his face and he chuckled.

"Truth be known Sam, I guess I'm glad you're here. Things are going to get bad when

those two gangs meet and I'll need you to watch my back." He looked at Sam's vest. "Where's your badge?"

"Same place as yours."

"With Thurston?" Tye asked. Sam nodded. "You mean to tell me Thurston knew of your following me?"

"Yup. He said I was to keep you out of trouble cause you were going to be like a little lost pup in the woods," Sam said laughing.

Tye laughed and reach out and shook Sam's hand. "Glad to have you with me pard. Now, we have a little daylight left so let's quit jawing and close the distance some on these outlaws."

Chapter Eight

August 30, 1874

Willie and his bunch had traveled as far as they had dared in the dark last night before making a cold camp. Once again Willie sent Brad back to check how far the Mexicans were behind them. Brad was his best man and one who could be as sneaky and sly as the fox and could appear and disappear like an Apache. He was a good man to have on your side and a bad one against you.

They were eating hard, cold biscuits and cold bacon when Brad suddenly appeared amongst them. The men stared at him like he was a ghost. No one had heard him approaching the camp and they were expecting him. He truly moved like the night breeze, barely making a sound.

He looked at Willie. “The Mexicans are only a half mile behind us,” he said in a low voice. “So we must be quiet as sound carries in these rocky hills,” he said sweeping his arms over his head. I think maybe it would be smart to keep moving.” He looked up at the night sky. “The moon will be up in a hour or so and with no clouds to block its light and the stars we should be ble to see well enough. Think maybe that’s what the Mex will do also.”

Will finished chewing his biscuit and washed it down with some water. Wiping his mouth with a dirty sleeve he nodded. “Been thinking the same thing myself. We’ll head out as soon as we can see a little ways and then we’ll check on them to see if they are following or camped.”

Brad took a biscuit and some bacon offered to him from Lester and sat on a rock eating, waiting on the moon. There was no palaver among the others. The only sound was that of the horses munching on the short grass.

~~

Tye and Sam, lying behind some sage on the top of a hill looked down on the Mexican camp. Since the Mexicans where the ones chasing and not the ones being chased they had a couple of small fires going and lots of talk and laughter could be heard. The talk was Mexican and both Tye and Sam had a limited understanding of the language, but quickly figured out most of the talk concerned women and things the men had done with them or were going to do. *Pretty much like camped with a bunch of soldiers,* Tye thought to himself and chuckled. He started to tap Sam on the shoulder and start back down the hill the way they had come, but stopped when the men started scurrying around in the camp.

Sam whispered. "Looks like they are fixing to mount up and ride out."

Tye, looking up said. "They were waiting on the moon." They headed back down to their mounts knowing this would be a sleepless night and also realizing that Willie and his gang just might get caught sleeping.

~~

Brad, who had hung back from the others now caught up with them. "They are coming also," he said to Willie and Lester. Willie nodded.

"Its time," he said.

"Time for what?" Lester asked.

"Time to hole up and dry gulch these bastards and make a bone orchard of this place." He looked around and like what he saw. Where they sat on their horses was a flat area with no cover for thirty or so yards to either side except some cactus and small sage brush that was no more than three foot high and would not stop a bullet. There were large boulders farther away on both sides they could get behind.

"Rufus," Willie said. "Take the horses and walk them on ahead of us and find a place you can hold them till the shooting is over." Rufus started to argue that he wanted to stay and help kill the greasers, but thought again about what might happen if he questioned one of Willie's orders. The men dismounted and he took the reins of the horses and led them away.

"Brad, you take Ben, James, and Jarrod over yonder to those rocks and get yourself hid," he said pointing with his rifle. "Lester, you and Jarrod get in those over there," he said pointing to the opposite side of where the others would be. He added, "Make damn sure your Henry's are fully loaded and when I open up, fire as fast as you can and keeping firing till they ain't a Mex left in the saddle."

"Where you gonna be?" Lester asked.

"Right there," Willie answered pointing in the direction Rufus had gone with the horses. I'm gonna step out in front of them and shoot the man in front. That's yall's signal to open up." The men scattered like Willie told them to do and he walked ahead a few yards to a large rock and squatted down behind it. No more than ten minutes passed when the sound of horse's hooves striking rocks could be heard. Willie smiled and cocked his rifle. *It was greaser killin' time.*

Tye and Sam were no more than three hundred yards behind the bandits when Tye pulled up and dismounted.

“What’s going on, Tye?” Sam whispered.

Tye was walking around and kneeling every once in a while. “Willie and his boys were camped here and then moved on. I got a feeling they knew the Mexicans were on the move and they broke camp just a few minutes before Mendoza got here.” He walked back to Sandy and mounted. I got a feeling that Mendoza is fixing to get a warm welcome. They had not started moving when it sounded like a war ahead of them suddenly could be heard.

Willie stepped out from behind the rock startling the banditos. He already had the Henry to his shoulder and he fired at the nearest Mexican. Which was Mendoza. The bullet bore into his chest right above where the bandoliers. The force of the forty-four shell from twenty feet away somersaulted him backwards off his horse and he hit the rocky ground hard. He tried to reach for his pistol but his arms felt heavy and he could not move them. He tried to rise himself up but even lifting his head was impossible. He blinked his eyes and saw one of him falling off his horse and he realized he had been shot himself. He tried to cry out, but no sound would come . He thought *Mother of Mary I...*and he died.

As soon as Willie fired all hell had broken loose. Muzzle flashes lit up the area as Willie's men opened up. Some horses reared throwing their riders and others snorted and whinnied stomping their hooves frightened of all the sudden noise. Other screamed in pain as bullets hit them as well as their riders. Half of the men went down immediately, but these were fighting men and those not hit left their saddles and hit the ground firing their pistols as they did. They put up a valiant fight but it was hopeless as they had no cover other than dead horses to get behind and even then they were in crossfire. Still, they returned deadly, accurate fire for a couple of minutes, then it was over. There was silence in the little canyon except for the nickering and whinnying of a couple of wounded horses. Willie stood up and walked among the carnage. Twelve men were down and all but two of the horses were dead or wounded. He took his pistol and put them out of their misery.

One by one his men came out of the rocks. Willie looked at each and realized Lester wasn't among them. He rushed over to where his brother had been and saw him crumpled on the ground. "No," he shouted and knelt quickly beside him. Turning him over and scared what he would find he was relieved to see a bloody furrow on the left side of his head just above the ear. He was alive by half an inch. The bullet had burned him and he was barely conscious, but he was alive.

Willie stood up and looked at the men who had gathered around him. "Where's Ben?"

"He bought it Willie," Brad said. "He caught one in the throat and died hard."

"Damn," Willie cursed. "Brad you help me here with Lester. The rest of you make sure none of those bastards are still alive." He and Brad lifted Lester and propped up up against a boulder. They heard a shot and looked up knowing that one of the men found a live Mex which was now a good Mex- a dead one. They saw Rufus coming back with the horses.

"Brad," Willie said softly. "Would you bring my saddle bags? I've got some stuff I can use on Lester's wounds."

A few minutes later Lester slouched on his horse, head bandaged and barely conscious. Willie looked at Rufus. "Ride beside him and make sure he stays in the saddle. We've got to get shuck of this place," he said looking at the others. "With all the shooting the Federales may be coming to take a look-see and I don't want to be around if they do." He reined his horse around and continued west, deeper into Mexico.

Tye and Sam had witnessed the fight, or slaughter if one wanted t call it that, and for the first time saw the nature of the men they were chasing.

"GawdAlmighty, Tye," Sam exclaimed. "I never saw anything like that in my whole life. They killed every damn one of those Mex in less than a minute."

Tye was amazed also. Had seen it before but it was Apaches killing soldiers in ambushes, not white men doing the killing. *This is a bad bunch,* he thought. *That was as slick of an ambush as I ever saw before. Then walking around making sure they were all dead.* He shook his head. "I knew they were some bad hombres, but..."his voice trailed off. He looked at Sam. Let's get our horses and get after them. If there are any soldiers around I don't want any part of them.

As they rode through the ambush site Tye saw Mendoza lying on his back, his unseeing eyes staring up at the sky. Tye felt for him and his men. He wondered what had sent the man off on the outlaw trail. So far in his two years of marshaling he had learned that just about every outlaw he had encountered had his reasons for being the way he was. For some it was a brutal father; for others it was the war and all the killing they had done and seen; for some it was being abandoned by parents or their parents being killed when they were young and had to whatever to survive. Some though were just born mean and rode with the devil. He wasn't sure what caused Willie and Lester to become what they were but he knew for a fact, Satan himself was now riding with them and he figured no way on earth was he going to be able to bring them in alive...even he wanted to- which he didn't.

Chapter Nine

August 31, 1874

With the killing of Mendoza and his gang Willie and his men felt pretty damn safe. They sat on their played out mounts looking at a fair sized town ahead of them about a mile. Willie sat with his hands crossed and resting on the saddle horn of his saddle.

“These horses need some rest and some grain so we’ll see if we can find us a couple or so rooms and hole up for a couple days,” Willie said. “I’ll only say this one time; any one of you gets in a ruckus or cause’s anyone to take notice of us I will personally shoot him. You get too much whiskey and get a leaky mouth you might as well shoot yourself because I sure as hell will shoot your ass." He turned and looked at Rufus. "Yours and Ben's need for a poke ended up getting Ben killed and my brother shot has done soured my belly so what I just said goes double for you."

Rufus swallowed and in a voice expressing his sorrow said. "Ben was my best friend, Willie. No one is more upset about what happened than me."

"You just keep that damn pecker in your pants-understood," Willie growled. Rufus nodded his head. "Let's go then," Willie said.

They entered the town from the east and it was bigger than it had appeared at first. From where they sat earlier they could only see about one third of the town, village, or whatever the Mexicans called them. As they rode in Willie nodded to the right and all saw the two men in uniforms standing guard at a building with ***La Policia*** painted on a sign above the door. Both of them watched the gringos as they passed.

Taking a glance back, Willie saw only one was still at the door. *The other one must be telling his superior all about us gringos,* Willie mused. He turned in the saddle and in a low voice said, “You boy’s seen those police back there. Well, one of them left his post and is telling his superior officer about us so I’m reminding you again-no trouble.”

A few minutes later they found a building with *Caballeriza* painted in faded letters which translated in english as stables. “Stay here while I talk to the owner,” Willie said. Walking into the building he was surprised at how clean and neat it was. The stalls looked clean with hay and the place only smelled faintly of horseshit. Only four of the stalls had horses in them. A little old man with a wrinkled face that made him look a hundred years old came out of what Willie figured was the tack room. His hair was white as snow and hung down to his shoulders.

“Speak English?” Willie asked.

“Si, Senor. A little.”

We have seven horses that we need bedded down, fed and watered for a couple days.” The old man rubbed his chin and smiled. Willie saw that he probably didn't have four teeth in his whole damn head.

"Lets see," the old Mexican said puckering his lips and obviously counting the dollars in his head. "Three dollars and fifty cents per day for all seven," he finally said.

"Willie smiled and handed him a ten dollar gold piece. 'This is for two days. You can keep the change." He walked outside and told the others to bring their horses and his around to the back which they did. Each man unsaddled his horse and threw his blanket and saddle in the tack room. They took their rifles and saddlebags and walked outside. A short distance down the street the word *Posada* was painted on a building and next to it a cantina. "That's damn handy," Willie said. "A hotel next to a bar." They all laughed as they strode toward the hotel to get a room ad a maybe a hot bath.

Tye and Sam sat in the same spot the outlaws had earlier and studied the town.

"Looks peaceful enough," Sam noted.

"Looks can be deceiving," Tye said. "If Willie and his bunch are there you can count on something happening and it won't be good," Tye replied. "Let's ride in and take a look-see and see if those varmints stayed or passed on thru."

The two men rode slowly pass the building with **La Policia,** painted on it and both men nodded to the two uniform men by the door as they passed. They rode to the livery and Sam dismounted and went inside and was back out in less than a minute.

"Their horses are in there, Tye. The old Mex that runs this place said seven gringos came in and paid in advance for one day for all the horses. He watched them get rooms and after bathing went into the cantina."

"How did he know all this?"

Sam chuckled. "Seems his brother owns the hotel and cantina and he sent a boy to ask the old man if they stabled their horses with him."

"I could use a drink. How about you, Sam?"

Sam looked at Tye like he had been smoking loco weed. "You want to go in there with seven men, seven killers, seven loco son-of-a bitches."

"Yep," Tye answered. "It's time we seen what they look like without them knowing who we are. Maybe we can sit close enough to them to get an idea of what they are going to do or where they are going. Just take it easy like and don't get riled over anything they say-if they say anything to us. Just put a hobble on your lip and listen for anything they say that might be useful later."

"I hope like hell you know what you are doing," Sam replied. "My pappy told me once that only a fool puts his head in bear's jaws and expects not to get bitten."

Tye smiled and put his hand on his friends shoulder. "There won't be any bears in there."

Sam forced a smile and thought. *No bears, only seven crazy bastards that have killed thirteen or so men in the last week. What's two more?*

Chapter Ten

The two lawmen entered the cantina and walked straight to the bar after letting their eyes adjust to the dimness inside. Both men noticed the men at the two tables all turn their heads and quickly took a look at them. Tye and Sam made it a point not to glance their way. They stood at the bar and ordered two mugs of beer. When the old Mexican with a apron on that was probably at one time white brought them Tye flipped four bits on the bar.

Lifting the mug to his lips Tye looked in the dirty mirror on the wall in front of him and quickly saw the men had gone back to talking among themselves-probably about him and Sam.

"Let's get a table Sam," Tye said just loud enough for the men to hear. They strolled over to a table and sat down. The table was against the back wall and Tye took a chair with his back to the wall and Sam sat where he was facing the tables where the men sat. A quick look showed the men were paying no attention to them.

A minute later potential trouble walked in. An officer and three uniformed men came in. The officer was a fat slob of a man with a handlebar mustache that was over size. He wore a spotless uniform with about ten pounds of medals and emblems on his chest.

"Bet he bought all that brass he's wearing," Sam whispered.

Tye chuckled quietly. "If he earned them it must have been years ago."

The man glanced at Tye and Sam and then walked directly to the two tables where Willie and his men sat.

In a pompous, loud voice and strutting like a rooster the officer stopped next to Willie. The distinct click of rifles being cocked caused all eyes to go to the three policeman. They stood with their rifles cocked and pointed in the general direction, but not at the tables. “May I ask the nature of you men’s visit to our humble town?”

In a very friendly like tone Willie answered. “We’re just passing thru. Our horses were plum tuckered out and we want to let them rest up a bit and then we’ll be on our way. We sure don’t want no problems.”

“I understand about your horses. It seems like every time a large group of gringos ride in to our humble little town there is trouble and most don’t ride out.”

Willie held up his hands and said in the most sincere voice he could muster. ”We sure don’t want any problems with you or your men. We just want to eat, drink a little beer and tequila and rest up before going on our way.”

“Very well, senor. Have a good time. But know that we will be watching.” He turned and walked to the door and gave a command in Spanish and the men un-cocked their rifles and followed him out.

"Cocky little bastard wasn't he?" Willie mumbled.

"Someone ought to take the fat slob and bring him down off his high horse," Rufus said. "I sure as hell don't like being bulldozed."

"Pull in your horns Rufus," Willie said sharply. "Just drink your beer quit flapping your lip. All of you be quiet fpr a minute or two. I got me some thinking to do."

"Whatcha thinking, Tye?" Sam asked in a soft voice.

"Just thinking I'm glad Willie has some smarts. The others might have taken offense to the Mex and started a ruckus that they would not win. I'd be willing to bet that he had several more men outside just for that purpose," Tye whispered. He stood up and strolled to the window and pulled the dirty curtain back and looked out. Several uniformed men were marching away. He walked back toward his table but stopped by Willies. "Glad you handled that situation the way you did mister. They had nigh on twenty other men on foot outside the cantina in case you made a foolish move."

Willie didn't answer, just nodded. After Tye walked away and sat down with Sam, Willie spoke in a low voice.

"Any of you know that feller?" No one spoke up for a moment then Brad answered.

"Never saw him before, but you can tell he's mucho hombre and a man you would not want to tangle with by his looks and the way he moves. His partner looks like he's someone to ride the river with. Just lookin' them over, I'd say they were two you didn't want to tangle with unless you had to."

"Bout the way I sized them up too," Willie said.

"Let's get out of here, Sam," Tye said loud enough for all to hear. "We got a long ways to go." Both men downed the last of their beer and walked outside not acknowledging Willie and his bunch.

Outside, they mounted their horses and were walking them out of town Sam spoke up. "How come we just didn't get the drop on them yahoos and disarm them while they were all bunched up at the tables."

"The thought crossed my mind, but those hombres ain't gonna surrender their guns and there would have been gun play and with seven to two odds, chances are one or both of us was taking a hit. If we succeeded in coming out alright how long do you think it would take for Mr. Brass buttons to get here with his men." He paused for long second and added. "I want to take them out yonder away from people."

"That idea shines with me." They rode in silence for awhile before Sam asked. "Where we going anyway?"

"Don't rightly know till we get there," Tye replied. "Look for a place along the trail we can set up a little surprise for them."

They had rode for about five miles when they rounded a bend in the trail and were suddenly face to face with four Mexicans who from their looks were bad hombres. Both groups reined up and studied each other. The four had bandoliers across their chest, Colts on their hips and rifles in their saddle leather. They stopped about thirty feet from Tye and Sam. One of the Mexicans, probably the leader Tye figured, stepped his horse forward a couple of steps. He was a heavy set man with a full beard that needed trimming badly. He wore a black sombrero with a lot of silver designs, a dirty blue shirt

Tye whispered to Sam. “If this goes the way I figure, start shooting at the one on the left and move to the right. I’ll start on the right and move to the left.” Tye shifted his butt around and quickly removed the leather thong holding his gun in its holster without being obvious. Sam didn’t have a leather thong holding his in.

“Ha! Gringos,” the leader with a big smile splitting that showed several missing teeth said. He raised his left arm and swept in front of him, “What are you doing in this beautiful country of mine?”

Tye whispered again. “If he takes his sombrero off and places in his lap draw and start firing.” He looked at the Mexican. “Just passing through.”

“I think you need to pay to travel in my country gringo.”

"Didn't know anyone owned this land except the Mexican government," Tye said. He knew that no matter what he said now, there was going to be gun play. This bunch was on the shoot.

The Mexican took off his sombrero. He wiped his face with his sleeve. "It's going to be hot today, I think."

"Get ready," Tye whispered.

The Mexican dropped the sombrero in his lap and Tye and Sam drew at the same time. Both Colts fired as one and heavy forty-four caliber slugs hit the two outside Mexicans square in the brisket. Both men grunted and hit the hard ground. Tye fired again but the man that had been doing the talking horse jumped sideways at the sound of the guns and he missed. Sam fired again and missed and two bullets cut the air close to Tye's head. He feathered the trigger again and saw a puff of dust on the leader's chest. Sam fired again and the other outlaw toppled backwards off his horse. Both men held their guns level waiting to see if anyone of them was still alive.

When it was obvious they were all dead Sam ejected the spent shells and reloaded as Tye was doing. "How did you know about the sombrero trick?"

"Damn near got my head shot off once awhile back by a Mex using that trick. I guess it's a common practice over here with the hard cases."

"I'd be dead as a piece of old wood if you hadn't said something about it. That Mex would have had his gun out before I was even aware he was going to draw."

"Something to remember Sam." He looked at the Western sky. "Going to be dark in about an hour. Let's see if we can find a place to hole up and keep a watch on our friends here."

"Why in tarnation do you want to watch over some dead people?"

"I think our friends back in town may feel their welcome is about over and will move out in the morning. Don't you suppose they may stop here and wonder what the

Sam hill happened? If we are close enough we can knock down a couple of them and then skedaddle before they can figure out what the blazes is going on."

"Why not get more than a couple?"

"Because I want them to fret over who it is killing them. I want them to suffer some for what they have done. I've never dry gulched any man in my life, but I'm gonna make an exception this one time."

They rode only a few yards when Tye reined Sandy left end made his way up an old deer trail that cut through the brush and rocks. He found a place about seventy yards off the trail that had good cover and an excellent view of the dead Mexicans about sixty yards below them.

"This will do," Tye said as he dismounted. He took his bedroll from behind the cantle of his saddle and spread it on the ground. Sam did the same. They gathered a little dry wood, started a fire and put some water on to boil for coffee. Sam got a skillet and dropped in some sowbelly. In a few minutes they were drinking coffee, eating bacon and dipping biscuits in the hot grease. They were through eating by dark and sat on their bedrolls listening to the night sounds.

"Night sky looks the same, night sounds are the same," Sam said, then added. "Can't tell this country form Texas, but I sure have a hankering to get back to familiar territory."

Tye chuckled. "I know what you mean, but I ain't leaving till every one of those murdering bustards is dead." He was quite for a moment then said softly. "I just wish I knew if Buff's okay.

"You put a lot of store in that old codger don't you?"

Tye nodded. "I love that old man like he was my own grandpa. He's my only link to my pa. He's told me a hundred stories about pa and his adventures back in the Rockies that pa never told me."

"Why do you suppose your pa didn't tell you."

"Pa," Tye said smiling, "Wasn't a man to toot his own horn. From what Buff said, he was every bit the mountain man Bridger was, but he just wasn't no braggart.

I'm not saying Bridger was, but Bridger liked to talk to anyone who would listen especially those men who wrote those dime novels. Pa had some wrote about him too, but only because Buff would bend one of those writers ear every now and then and sic them onto pa at the yearly rendezvous. I wish I had been there to see what those men saw. It had to be a strange feeling to look upon a land no man had laid eyes on before-at least no white man." No words were spoken for a few moments as both men thought about the things they had heard about the Rockies. "You ever were up north to the mountains?"

"Can't say I have. Biggest I ever saw were those up around Ft. Davis."

Tye laughed. "Buff came down to Clark through those mountains. He laughed when we asked him what he thought of them. He would laugh and say, 'Sonny, those there montons wudn't even be futhills in them there Rockies."

"Danged if you don't sound just like old Buff."

"If you hung around him long enough you would talk a little different too. The mountain men had a strange but colorful way of talking. Buff said it was a mixture of English and French with a whole lot of made up words throwed in.

The fire died out and eventually the coals also as did the talk and the camp settled in for the night.

~~

Back in the village Willie was turning things over in his mind. A couple of the boys were becoming a little bit roostered up and he was afraid they might cause a ruckus if provoked by any of the Mex that was in the bar. There were a few tough looking hombres in the crowd of mostly town folk who were dressed in their white shirts and pants.

Willie made up his mind. The longer he stayed the chances went up of there being trouble. The hombres that were obviously not locals kept looking their way.

"Brad, take Rufus and go saddle our horses."

"What's up boss?" Brad asked.

"I got me a feeling if those hombre's at that table in the corner get any more lickkered up we could have problems and with that damn highfalutin' son-of-a-bitch officer just waiting for us to make a wrong move we could be knee deep in trouble real quick. Now get to it and get them horse saddled." The two men stood up and left with Brad sorter holding Rufus, who never could hold his liquor, upright walked through the doors.

Five minutes later Willie nudged Lester with his elbow to get his attention. "Go to our rooms and get the saddlebags and take them to the livery. Put them on the horses and then you, Brad, and Rufus bring the horses to the front of the cantina and wait for us."

After his brother had left Willie finished his beer and sat looking at the three Mexicans sitting at the corner table. The more he studied on the situation the more he figure the three were with the two that sat at a table nearby. He noticed that none of the five had their backs to him which made him even more sure they were looking for trouble.

Fifteen minutes passed and Willie, James, Jarrod and Billy stood up and started for the door. They were almost to it when one of the Mex in the corner spoke in a loud voice. "Hey gringos. Where you go? It is early yet and the music and the girls will be here shortly." Then he added. "Or maybe you cowboys rather go make love to one of your cows."

Jarrod, standing to Willies left, moved his hand toward the butt of his gun but Willie grabbed it and held it. Willie laughed. "You are right, we had rather make love to a cow than the ugly whores you have around here you piece of shit greaser." As the last word came out of his mouth he pulled his Colt and fired. The forty-four caliber slug struck the mouthy Mexican in the chest just about where the third button was just as he was digging for his cannon. The locals were scattering tables and turning over chairs as they hit the floor just as the other three men with Willie opened up with their Colts spewing deadly fire. Only one of the Mexicans was able to get up from his chair, pull his gun and fire before two slugs tore into him knocking him into the wall and hanging there for a long second before sliding to the floor dead as the wood he lay on.

Willie had heard a grunt and saw James crumpled to the floor holding his shoulder. Willie, looking through the thick smoke from the Colts saw all the Mex were down. About that time Lester came through the door gun in his hand. Willie said. "Grab James and help him into his saddle and all of you get mounted. Willie held his gun level covering the patrons of the cantina before backing out and jumping onto his horse and taking the reins from Lester.

"Time to cut and run." He shouted and headed out of town. The bad side of this country if you were an outlaw was that the terrain directed your travel. There was just not too many ways a man could go on a horse. If you were a lawman, that was a good thing cutting down the options a outlaw had to travel. Willie and his men were on the road toward their first meeting with a man they didn't really want to meet.

Chapter Eleven

Sept 1, 1874

It was well after midnight when Tye awoke suddenly. He lay there listening and heard what had awaken him- the sound of horses hooves and several of them on the rocky ground. He nudged Sam.

"Horses coming," he said grabbing his Henry and moving over to the edge of the cliff and peering down. Sam slid in beside him.

"Who is it? He whispered.

"Looks like the Mills brothers and his bunch. One of them looks like he's hurt." Tye answered.

“What the hell!” he heard one of the men swear as they came on the bodies of the Mexicans. They all sat their horses looking down at the bodies.

“What do you supposed happened to them?” Jasper asked. Tye and Sam could hear the voices but not every word till Willie spoke up.

“I bet these jaspers met those two cowboys that were in the cantina. I told you they looked like curly wolves,” and I was right.

“Pick you a target. Sam,” Tye whispered. Just don’t shoot Willie. “Let’s open the dance pard,” he said as he squeezed off a shot from his Henry. Sam’s shot followed Tye’s by a second and two men were blown from the saddle. Before the echo of the rifles shots had faded, the two lawmen were moving to and mounting their horses. Tye had already scouted a way down the mountain other than the way they had come and would put them about a mile farther up the trail than where they had left it earlier. Before they left Tye left a note he had written earlier and left it on a boulder with a small rock holding it in place.

Willie—We could have shot you and Lester, but I'm saving you two for last. Especially you Willie boy.

TW

Willie and the four remaining outlaws had hit the ground and scrambling for cover as soon as the shots were fired. Rufus and James lay on the ground, neither moving.

"Anybody see where those shots came from?" Willie asked.

"I saw flashes from up there," Brad said, "High and to the left." The men lay there several minutes before Willie stood up. "They've gone. Jarrod, you check on Rufus and James. "Brad, you come with me and let's take a look where those bastards were shooting from.

It took them a few minutes to reach the spot from where the shots were fired. Brad picked up a shell casing and smelled of it. He nodded. "This is the spot."

"What the hell!" Willie exclaimed. "Lookee here at this," he said handing the note Tye had written to Brad. "Whatcha make of that?"

Brad read the note. "I'd say we got a real problem."

Willie let out a curse and crammed the note in his pocket, then took it back out and looked at it again. "Who the hell is TW?"

"Dunno," Brad said then remembered something. "That bartender said that woman we were talking about was the wife a of bad ass hombre. Wasn't his name Tye something or other?"

"Watkins, I think it was," Willie said looking at the hills around him for any sign of a shooter.

"You reckon that's what that TW stands for, Tye Watkins?"

"That don't wash, Brad. Why would he be after us way over here in Mexico. We didn't hurt her none."

"Remember the old man with her. You ran over him with your horse on the way out of town. I bet he's some relative, maybe even his pa. Maybe he was hurt real bad or even killed."

Willie sat down on a rock. "That has to be it and I bet that big varmint in the cantina yesterday was him." He let out a curse, “Damn, we should have found a reason to kill him then. He knows what each of us look like now so they won’t be no foolin’ him any if we meet again somewhere.”

Brad chuckled. “Since when did you need a reason to kill some hombre.“ Then in a more somber tone said.”If what that barkeep said about him there won’t be no quit in him till we are dead-or he is.”

“Well if he thinks he will have me running skeerd he’s wasting his time. Been long ago since Willie Mills was afraid of any man.”

“Didn’t know you were ever skeerd of any man Willie.”

“Only one,” Willie said. “And I killed him.”

“Who was that?”

“My pa.”

“You killed your pa?”

“Sure as hell did and I wish I could do it again.” He took another look around and started back down the hill to the others. Brad followed wondering what would cause a man to kill his own father.

~~

Tye, along with Sam, squatted on their heels chewing some hard tack and washing it down with warm water from their canteens. They were behind some scrub oak and a bush with a hell of lot of thorns on it which Sam was bellyaching about as he pulled a thorn out of his hand.

"Acacia," Tye said.

"What?" Sam asked.

"Those bushes I believe are Acacia. Pa told me once they have a lot of medicinal uses."

"Yeah, I can believe that. A man needs some caring for if he gets to damn close to one of them. They're worse than the damn mesquite and cactus back home which by the way you have here also in abundance. Every stinking bush or tree here can scratch you or stick you. Makes a fellow feel right at home," he chuckled.

"Sam," Tye said in a serious tone of voice. "Did shooting those two men back there like that bother you some?"

"Some, I guess." Sam looked out over the vast emptiness before him pondering what to say next then spoke. "But not enough to prevent me from doing it again to the likes of those varmints."

"I've killed a lot of men, Sam," Tye saw in a somber voice. "Couldn't even begin to guess how many counting Indians." He picked up a pebble and pitched it up a couple times and catching it in his palm. "Of all those men, not once have I ever killed one that wasn't shooting at me, trying to kill me until today. I didn't think it would bother me considering what they have done, but I was wrong." He threw the pebble away."

"What are we gonna do then? We just can't take on five hombres that are meaner than a curly wolf straight on and hope we can outshoot them."

" We'll figure something out pard." Tye changed the subject. "You've seen me draw and I want you to give me an honest answer. I've put in a lot of work the last couple years so tell me ,am I'm fast enough to stand up face to face in a gunfight?"

"Hell yes you're fast. I'm pretty handy when it comes to drawing and shooting and you're quicker than me." If you want the straight of it, you're probably the quickest I've ever seen and I've seen mor'n a few. "But," he said, "I've only seen you in practice. There's a hell of lot of difference when you're standing before some outlaw that has his mind set on killing you." I don't know what you have in mind or what you are planning, but don't get yourself all balled up thinking what we did was wrong in shooting those two men. It's the only way without one or both of us getting shot up." No one spoke for a minute then Sam added."Aw hell," he chuckled. "Truth be known, I just don't want to see you get killed cause I'd never find my way back to Texas." Both men laughed.

"Give me the straight of it on what you think of this. We'll find a place where you can have a clear killing area from behind some brush, rocks or some sort of cover. It'll be a place where I can stay out of sight till they are right on me and I'll step out and ask them to shuck their guns. With me in front and you on one side of them with that Henry we should have them pretty well covered."

"And you're gonna step out with your gun holstered?"

"No. Won't lie to you and say I didn't think about it, but I'll have my gun out.

"There's only one problem I can see with that." Sam said. "They ain't gonna back down and shuck those guns. Those boys ain't no yellow belly cowards and they would rather die standing than give up. That the way I see it." He paused to let what he said sink in. "Tye, you are probably the best, most honorable man I have ever met, but the bone orchard is full of honorable men lying there. I will do it whatever way you want, but these men are the worse of any I have seen and I've been around a lot more than you in this marshaling business. They would not give me or you a break in any way. I had an old ranger tell me one time that the only way to survive this law business is to be as mean and low down as the men you are chasing. If you are not, you ain't gonna last long. I took that to heart and I'm here and a lot of them are pushing up daises. Ole Buff told me that the only worry he has with you is sometimes you just try to be too damn fair."

Tye sighed. "You're probably right about them hombres not giving up and there would be gun play."

"This is the way I see things, Tye, and I know you may not agree with the way I look at things sometimes. These hard cases are men who have done things to people, robbed, raped, and killed, that no normal man would ever dream of doing. They have destroyed a lot of families and unless we stop them they will continue doing just that very thing. As far as I'm concerned they should be hunted down and shot the same way one would do with a rabid dog. That's the way I see it and if we kill every one of them I won't lose a minute of sleep over it." They sat there for a full minute no one saying anything then Sam said laughing. "Course we could we could just ask them in a nice way to just give up and then both of us would get plenty of sleep-permanent like."

"Sam, we've worked together for what, two years now? I believe you have just said more words in the last five minutes than you have in all that time," Tye said laughing. “But you are right and Buff is right. Sometimes I let fair play go a little far. I remember about five years ago when the captain of a patrol I was scouting for chased some Apaches while I was way out in front and got him and his men ambushed. I arrived in time to help pull them out but damn near got killed doing it. I was on a bluff above the Apaches hidden in the rocks that were shooting down on the trapped men. I took a bead on the nearest braves back and hollered because I didn’t want to shoot him in the back. Well sir, that Apache twisted around so fast it surprised me and he snapped off a shot which whistled by my ear before I shot him. That should have taught me a lesson but I guess I’ve always been a little pig headed about things.”

“Never knew that,” Sam replied laughing.

“We’ll do it your way Sam-with one difference. We’ll find a place where we can get them in a crossfire. I’ll ask them one time to throw their guns down and surrender which, as you said, they won’t do and the dance will be open.”

"I can set with that plan," Sam said then added a line that had both of them laughing so hard tears were in their eyes. "When we throw down on them and they pull their hog legs it's gonna get hotter than a whorehouse on nickel night." When they quit laughing so hard he then added. "And that's pretty damn hot." Both broke into laughter again.

Regaining his composure Tye said. "You know Sam I don't know where in blazes you come up with some of these things you come up with."

"Man's gotta be good at something I guess." They both laughed again.

Tye stood up and stretched the kinks out of his body. "Let's mosey down the trail and find a spot and get this over with."

Chapter Twelve

Mid morning Sept 1, 1874

Lester had been rattled some ever since Willie told him and the others about the note. He was constantly looking at the hills, bushes, rocks, and every other place that a man might hide behind. In private Willie told him to calm down and they might just get lucky and kill this Watkins feller. “Remember,” he said, “the note says me and you are last so quit worrying and be ready to kill the man when he fires at one of the others.” Willie was riding with his Colt in his hand.

Brad, Jarrod, and Billy were riding behind the brothers. In fact, they were riding as close as they could get. Willie turned around and wasting no words told them to spread out and not make it so damn easy for the bastard to shoot everyone. "Aint no sense in making it like shooting fish in a damn barrel," he shouted.

The men spread out with Billy and Jarrod farthest back. Billy whispered. "He might not be so damn high and mighty ifin' he was in our place and was told he was in line first to be shot. I kno whut he's thinkin'. When that feller shoots at us, he and Lester might have a chance to shoot him. Wal, I don't kno about you, but I don't hanker much to being a damn target."

"Looks to me like we're up the creek with no paddle," Jarrod said softly. "If we stay there's a good chance this Watkins feller will kill us, but ifin' we make a break, Willie will for certain. I think we stay and keep a sharp eye out and guns loose. Maybe we can get lucky and kill the son-of-a-bitch fore he does us."

Billy wasn't so sure about his chances. He had a bad feeling about things for days, ever since the incident in

Brackett. He had turned twenty-one recently and wanted to live a few more years, wanted to see what life was all about. So far his life had been full of trouble starting in school when he was always in fights. Reflecting back, he knew most of the trouble was his fault because of his temper. He was smaller than most other boys and seemed to always be the brunt of jokes. He took a lot of whippings from the bigger boys, but the constant fighting taught him one thing over time-he became a good fighter and eventually could whip the bigger boys and the taunting stopped.

The years of struggle and fighting taught him people respected a man who could fight and fear was an ally. When he was fifteen he ran away from home. He swamped saloon floors, worked in a livery cleaning horse shit out of the stalls, did a lot of trivial jobs and again was the brunt of jokes, but from men this time instead of boys. Two brothers, James and Bill Williams, were the worst of the bunch that hung out in the saloon. Unknown to anyone, Billy had stolen an old Colt and gun belt from a drunk months earlier that had been thrown out of the saloon. He kept it hidden under his bunk in the tack room in the livery.

Whenever he had time and no one was around he strapped on the gun and practiced drawing. He knew from listening to idle talk around the saloon that a gun fighter was greatly respected among folks. Respect, that was something he had never known and he wanted it badly.

Practice, practice, practice. Eventually, he thought himself to be pretty good though he had nothing to base his belief on. He had heard about gunfights, but had never actually seen one. He made up his mind that he was going to face down his worst antagonist. It happened unexpectedly.

One cold, miserable Saturday night in February he was sweeping the floors in the saloon when the Williams brothers walked in. They were in a worse mood than usual and were pretty much bullying everyone and then they spotted Billy. They started taunting him and broke a couple of empty bottles on the floor.

"Hey piss ant, clean this up too," James hollered. When Billy swept the broken glass into a pile and bent over to pick it up the other brother, Bill kicked him in the butt and he went sprawling on the floor. The two brothers howled with laughter along with a few of the men in the saloon, but the majority was silent not liking the way the boy was treated. The hoots grew louder when Billy picked himself up and walked out the door.

Five minutes later you could hear a pin drop in the saloon when Billy walked back in. Everyone immediately saw he was packing and wondered what the hell he was going to do. He stopped a few steps inside the door.

"James," he said, "You and Bill have had your fun with me for the last time. "

The two brothers looked at each other and started laughing. A few seconds later. Bill says in a slightly drunken voice, but loud enough for all to hear. "Brother, do you hear what I hear." He cocked his head to the side and cupped his hand around his ear. "I think I hear a namby-pamby piss ant of a boy who thinks he's a man because he has a hog leg strapped on. He stood up and walked a couple steps toward Billy. Chairs scraped the floor as men were getting out of the line of fire. As one, they all knew this youngster was fixing to breathe his last breath on this earth.

"Okay piss ant," Bill said. "What are you going to do, pull that piece or you going to piss in your pants."

Truth be known Billy was about to do that. He was scared, but he took a couple of deep breaths and it seemed to relax him a little bit. He looked over at a man he knew sitting at a nearby table. "Charlie," Billy said. "Count to three loudly." He looked at Bill. "On the count of three you had better draw."

Bill looked at James and back at the kid. "You serious?"

"Count Charlie," Billy said.

"One...two...three." Before the last sound of the word three sounded from Charlies mouth Billy drew and fired just as Bills gun was clearing leather. The forty-four slug hit the Bull Durham tag hanging from his shirt pocket. The big man staggered backwards a couple steps his gun falling from his fingers. He looked at his brother and then at Billy and fell face down on the floor. Billy holstered his gun and looked at James.

"Got anything to say, James." James looked down at his brother. His expression was one of surprise and also fear. The cigarette between his lips fell to the floor.

"You murdered by brother." He rushed to his brother and knelt beside him placing a finger on the side of his neck. There was no pulse. "You killed him in cold blood. All of you saw it," he shouted to the other men in the saloon."

Charlie spoke up. "Billy boy killed him alright James, but it was a fair fight. Bill was drawing his gun, but he wasn't fast enough. Young Billy here beat him fair and square with the fastest draw I ever did see."

"It's your turn James. I'm gonna make you pay like your brother did for all the things you have done to me that last few months." He waited a couple seconds then added. "Now stand up and draw or crawl out that door on your belly."

James whimpered. "I...I can't beat you. It would be murder." He looked at the other men, but saw no help in their faces. He started crawling out the door followed by the hoots and laughter of the men. Billy watched him till he got to the door and started to turn back to pick up his broom when a sudden shout warned him. He whirled around, drawing his Colt at the same time and fired once, twice. James had stood up at the door and then suddenly turned and was drawing his gun when the two bullets struck him in the chest knocking him out the door he had started to open. Men rushed over to him.

"Lookee here," one man said. "Them holes ain't an inch apart. The men looked at Billy who was still holding the smoking Colt.

"Ain't ever seen nothing like that," one said.

"Me neither," said another and on and on it went as one man after another either spoke or shook his head in amassment.

A minute later the sheriff came in with two deputies, guns drawn. He looked at the two dead men. "What the hell happened here?"

Charlie spoke up. "Wal sheriff, it seems like two ole boys that had been givin' a lot of shit to a certain youngster got their reward for their behavior tonight. It was a fair fight sheriff and young Billy boy there done slew the philistines. He called them out for all they had done to him and he smote them down like Samson done in the Good Book."

Sheriff Jennings looked at Charlie. "Since when did you start quoting from the Bible you old goat." Everyone laughed. "Now someone, other than preacher Charlie tell me what the hell happened."

After listening to several witnesses he told his deputies to get some help and carry the two bodies to the undertakers. He found an empty table and told Billy to sit down. "I can't say I blame you none for what you did Billy. Those two have had that coming for a long time, but their old man is a tough son-of-a-bitch and he's gonna come in here with some of his men off the ranch and he'll possibly hurt some innocent people in trying to get to you. You need to cut and run from this here town."

"I aint got no horse, no money or anything else cept the clothes on my back and my Colt. How am I gonna run?"

Everyone was listening to what was being said. Charlie stood up. "I got ten dollars Billy, you're welcome to it. This place here is going to be a lot quieter and more pleasant without those two and I thank you kindly fer it." He handed the ten dollar gold piece to Billy and before Billy could say thanks several more men gave him some money. Lester, the old coot that owned the livery said he had an old saddle and tack he would throw on a crowbait of a horse and give it to him.

"Looks like you're fixed up, Billy." Sheriff Jennings said. Billy stood up still not believing what was happening.

"You might as well have this Billy," the saloon owner said. He handed Billy a heavy coat. "James had it on the table. Don't think he'll be needing no coat where he's headed."

Billy thought some more as he rode beside Jasper about that night years ago. He had left that town with almost a hundred dollars, a horse and saddle, and a warm heavy coat and for the first time a little self respect. He wished now he could go back and change things that happened after that, but one can't change the past, only learn from it. He had slipped from being a somewhat decent human being to nothing but a killer, a man who only wants things other men have earned. It was a couple years after he killed the brothers that he figured out that a gun fighter's respect was based on fear, nothing else. The good folks wanted nothing to do with him and his only friends were men like him. He fell in with one bad crowd after another till he met the worst of the lot, Willie Mills. Now, it looked he was going to his reward for the life he had chosen-to hell and eternal damnation. For the first time in years, he thought of his ma and pa and wished he could turn back the pages of time.

Chapter Thirteen

It was noon when Tye found the place he was looking for. The shooter on the right would be forty yards from the trail and the shooter on the left about fifty yards. Easy range for a rifle but a tad long for a Colt at least for the normal cowboy. Tye knew these men were not normal cowboys and would not be ones that could not shoot center.

"What do you think?" Tye asked Sam.

Sam looked at both sides of the trail for a couple minutes. He saw the large number of huge boulders on the right. On the left side was a lot less cover but still enough to offer adequate protection for a man. He nodded. “Looks like as likely place as we’ll find.”

“Take your horse and get him situated deep in those rocks and then find you a good spot,” Tye said pointing to the boulders on the right. “I’ll do the same on the left.” They started in different directions to get situated, but Tye stopped. “Sam,” he said. “You keep your head down and don’t take any unnecessary chances. I don’t want to have to carry your sorry butt all the way back to Texas to bury you.” They both laughed.

Both men had their canteen’s and some jerky where they sat. Waiting-waiting for a fight was always the worse part. The fight, when it started was always a relief in a weird sort of way. Tye figured this fight would last maybe ten seconds or less. Longer than that could mean one or both of them taking a hit. The whole secret to a successful ambush was surprise and to knock men down with your first and second shots before they had time to react. If things went as planned it should be over quick. However, as Tye had learned over the years, in a fight very seldom do things go as planned.

Tye looked up at the sun. *It's a little after noon,* he thought. *I guess Rebecca is sitting on the porch full as a tick after one of her good meals. She's probably watching Little Ben and Nicole play.* Thinking of her and the kids brought a lump to his throat. *He loved her more today than he did when he married her and he will love her more tomorrow than he does today. And Ben and Nicole they were everything to him. Until they were born two years ago he never knew the depth of love a man could have for someone.* Another thought came to him. *I wonder about Buff. Buff meant more to me than I realized when I saw him lying injured and maybe dying in the post hospital. That old mountain man was as much a part of his family as anyone was.* He chuckled to himself remembering the first time Buff held Little Ben. It was the first time the old codger had ever held a baby and he couldn't figure out what position to put his arms in to do so. Since then he had become a first class grandpa loving those two kids like you couldn't believe. His thoughts were suddenly interrupted as the sound of horses coming struck his ears. He looked across the way and waved at Sam who waved back. It was time.

As Willie and his men came into sight Tye saw them rein in. They were still a hundred yards from where Tye and Sam waited. Tye could not figure what they were doing but it looked like they were looking at their back trail.

Willie was a wise old coon. He had been up the river and around the bend as men would say and he didn't like the way things looked ahead. He hadn't survived being captured or shot for so many years by being dumb. He studied the rocks ahead on both sides and knew it was a perfect place for Watkins to set up an ambush. He didn't relish going back the way they came as he figured someone had found the dead men they had shot and maybe the Federales were after him now. He had rather face two men than a whole damn patrol of Mexican police.

"I got a bad feeling about those rocks yonder," he said to his men pointing ahead. "If Watkins is there let's don't give him easy targets. Shake them hog legs out of their leather and be ready to shoot. Ride low and fast." He dug his spurs into his mounts flanks and the horse leaped forward. They lay low over the saddle as they came at Tye and Sam at a dead run.

Chapter Fourteen

Tye uttered an oath as he saw the men running their horses down the trail toward him and Sam. There was nothing he hated more than having to shoot a horse, but he was going to have to try and stop these men. He took sight on the lead horse and squeezed the trigger. The Henry belched the forty-four caliber slug and it struck the horse just below and in front of its left ear. The result was immediate as horse and rider went down hard. Tye saw another horse go down as Sam had done the same thing. The other horses slowed and tried to miss tripping on the ones on the ground. Tye fired again and the man in back did a back flip off his mount as the heavy slug hit him in the chest. Billy hit the ground hard and lay there, unable to move. It felt like a heavy weight was pressing on his chest, pressing the life out of him. It was hard to breathe and try as he might he couldn't lift his head from the ground. His face was pressed to the sand and his breath blew sand in the air as he struggled for air. "M...ma, I..." and he died.

Tye saw another man grab his throat with both hands as Sam's shot had apparently hit him there.. He stayed in the saddle for a few seconds as blood gushed between his fingers. A second shot from Sam blew him out of the saddle.

Tye ducked as a bullet from the remaining outlaw whizzed by his ear. He raised and fired quickly but missed. Another bullet ricocheted off a rock close to his face and rock fragments cut his cheek. He fired again and saw the outlaw double over and slowly slide from his saddle and hit the ground, one boot still in the stirrup. The horse, panicked from all the noise, trotted off dragging the man behind him.

One of the men who had gone down when his horse was shot came up firing at Sam. Tye shot him right between the shoulder blades and exploded out his chest. He pitched forward, dead before he hit the ground. Tye watched for a few more seconds to make sure no one moved before exposing himself. He waved at Sam and was very happy to see his partner wave back. Both men stood up and walked warily toward the men lying in the dust.

Sam caught the trotting horse and took the dead man's boot out of the stirrup. Tye checked the other men and all were dead except one-Willie. The outlaw leader had been knocked unconscious when his horse stumbled after being shot. Tye tied his hands together and then poured water on his face from his canteen.

Willie opened his eyes and shook his head throwing water everywhere. He saw Tye and tried to grab his gun and realized his hands were tied. He looked around and saw his brother lying close to him, his eyes and mouth open and a lot of blood on his chest.

“I’ll kill you,” he screamed. “You sorry piece of horse shit, I’ll kill you if it’s the last thing I ever do.”

Tye squatted on his heels in front of Willie. “You’ve killed your last man Willie. You’ve got one more trail to ride and that’s straight to the gallows and I am going to enjoy watching you swing.”

Willie spit in Tye’s face. Tye wiped the spittle off. In his mind he saw his friend Jim’s face with the bullet hole in his head; he saw Buff lying in the bed in the hospital almost dead; he saw Rebecca who could have been killed. He doubled up his right fist and hit the outlaw in the jaw with every ounce of strength he could muster behind it. All two hundred plus pounds of the outlaw was lifted off his feet and the first thing that hit the ground was the back of his head. He was out cold.

“Damn,” Sam said. “You might have killed the man.” In all his years, in all of the fights Sam had been in and witnessed, never had he seen a blow like the one that Tye just delivered.

“If it did, it will save the State of Texas a lot of time and money of a trial,” Tye said rubbing his bruised knuckles. “Let’s check the others again.” All were dead. They rummaged through the pockets of each man, removing cash and whatever papers they could find. They stripped each man of their gun belts and guns and carried the bodies to the rocks. They had no shovels so they gathered rocks and buried them under them to keep the varmints away. They were buried as they rode-together.

“Going to say any words over them, Tye?” Sam asked sweat running down his face.

Tye looked up at the sky and then at Sam. “Don’t figure it will help them one bit Sam. They’re on their way to their reward and I don’t figure it’s an upward path.”

Willie was coming around and sat up blinking and shaking his head trying to clear the cobwebs. “What happened?” he asked looking at Sam.

“I’d say you got kicked by a mule, but since they ain’t one of them around I’d guess you got slugged in the jaw by a very angry, upset man named Tye Watkins.

Willie looked around. “Where the hell is he?”

"Unsadding your men's horses and turning them loose."

"I don't know that man. Why did he have it in for me and my men? I never even saw him before."

"Back in Brackett," Sam said, "You shot the bartender. Well, that man happened to be one of Tye's best friends. The old man you ran over with your horse, he was Tye's best friend. He even lived with Tye. He was an old mountain man and was Tye's pa's best friend back in those days long ago. You and your men talked trash about Tye's wife and could have hurt her if the old man had not shoved her out of the way before you hit him. That's why Tye was after you and I'll tell you something else. When we get back, if that old man has died, you won't live to see the hangman, but you probably wish you did because what Tye will do to you will be worse than what any Apache would do to a white man." He stood up and added. "You and your men messed with the wrong hombre my friend."

Willie swallowed the lump in his throat. "Do you think he will kill me in cold blood."

Sam looked over his shoulder at Tye approaching. "If I was you I would be as quiet as a church mouse on the way back to Texas and not give him a reason to. I've seen what that man can do when he's riled and it ain't pretty."

"W...what's he do?" Willie asked.

"Whatcha mean by that?"

"Is he a rancher, or farmer or what."

Sam turned his head to prevent Willie from seeing his smile. "None of those. He just mostly kills men like you for the pure pleasure of it. Say's the world is a better place without vermin like you." Sam quit smiling and turned back to face Willie and with his most threatening voice. "Like I said, it would be smart not to rile him none."

Sam walked to meet Tye. "Everything okay?" Tye asked.

"Right as rain," Sam answered. "By the way, Tye," Sam whisperd. "I told him what a bad hombre you are and loved to kill vermin like him so play it tough."

"That won't be hard to do with that piece of horse dung." He walked over to where Willie sat and squatted on his heels in front of him. "I'm going to tell you something and you'd better take it as gospel. Men like you make me sick. You're too lazy to work so you take what other men have earned. You kill for the pure pleasure of it when there's no reason for doing it." All of a sudden, his Bowie was in his hand and he pressed into the skin under Willie's left eye drawing blood. Tye's eyes bulged, his face took on a crazy man expression and he let out a blood curdling Apache war hoop that even startled Sam. Willie fell onto his back. Tye stood over him his knife in Willie's face. "Just give me a damn reason-just one." He stood over an obviously shaken Willie for a few seconds then abruptly turned and walked away winking at Sam as he did.

Tye mounted Sandy and Sam mounted his horse after helping Willie on his.

"How about tying my hands in front so I can hold on to the horn in case we have to start running for some reason." Tye dismounted and pulled his Bowie while walking back to Willie. Willie, seeing the knife, broke out in sweat. Tye cut a piece of rope and made a loop in one end and stuck Willies right boot in it and pulled the loop tight. He threw the other end under the horse and tied it snugly to the man's left boot pulling it tight under the horse's belly. He slashed the ropes holding the outlaws hands behind his back and retied them in front. He looped the loose end around the saddle horn a couple times and snubbed it down.

"Don't take many chances does he?" Willie said to Sam after Tye walked away.

Sam snickered and said. "Told you to be careful about what you say and how you say it."

"I can set with that," Willie replied quietly. "That man is plumb loco."

Sam smiled. "Don't think we'll have a problem with Mr. Willie boy there," he whispered to his horse patting him on the neck.

An hour of traveling on the trail ended when Tye abruptly left the trail. Where he led was rough going. There was just an animal trail and it was a faint one.

Most men would not have paid it a second glance, but Tye learned a long time ago that animals, particularly deer, always found a way to go through brush, rocks, hills and gulley's, and it was usually fairly easy trail either leading to water or from water. Tye hoped this one led to water.

Willie was fifteen feet back of Tye and Sam was just behind Willie. Willie twisted as best he could with his hands being lashed to the saddle horn and asked in a low voice.

"Where in hell is he going? We could have lot easier riding on the main trail."

"Why don't you just ask him?"

Willie turned back in the saddle and thought to himself. *I'd rather ask the devil himself a question afore I ask that loco bastard anything. A lot can happen in the three days it's going to take us to get back to Bracket. I've just got to be ready when my chance comes.*

An hour later they were sitting their mounts looking over a small lake.

We can rest here and let the horses drink their fill," Tye said. He untied the rope from the horn and untied one end of the rope holding the outlaws feet. Willie looped his right leg over the horse's neck and slid to the ground.

"I need to take a piss," Willie said. "Can you untie my hands?"

"Just make do with your hands tied," Tye replied. Willie walked a few steps away mumbling under his breath. While Willie was relieving himself Tye walked over to Sam. We have about three hours daylight left. You two make yourselves comfortable for a little while. I'm going to scout ahead for a good trail through these hills. I don't hanker much to ride down the main trail we were on. I got a hunch the police are on to the trail by now."

Willie turned and walked back to them and Tye told him to sit which he did. He untied his hands and tied them behind his back and then tied his feet together. He mounted Sandy and rode off.

"Where's he think he's going?" Willie asked staring after Tye.

"Finding us a trail through the hills. Federales may be on the main trail after all the bodies we left scattered along it. Don't figure we want to tangle with them."

"Who the hell is this hombre? That barkeep in Bracket spoke of him like he was not a mortal man."

"Some say he may be. The Apache think he is special and have been trying to kill him for years. A lot of them are under the ground. At one time he rode with the Texas Rangers. He tracked down so many bandits they put a bounty on him. No one could collect it. He's an expert with a gun, knife, tomahawk, or any other weapon you can name. Hell, I've seen him damn near beat a man to death with his fists that was a hell of lot bigger than him and supposedly one bad-ass hombre. He's a man that a man like you doesn't want any part of." Sam took a pull on his canteen and and added. "Don't think you can get away either. Another thing he's good at is tracking and reading sign. Some of the soldiers at Fort Clark say he can track a lizard over rocks."

"Must be part Apache," Sam said spitting out the words.

"He can live off the land as well as they can. You saw how he found this here water hole." Sam looked Willie in the eye. "Willie, you might as well get set with the fact you're gonna hang or if you're lucky, piss Tye off and he'll kill you and you won't have to sit it the hoosegow waiting to get your neck stretched. Course you may not like the way he goes about killing you." He let the words sink in for a minute then added. "If 'in I was you I wouldn't get my back up and I'd keep a hobble on my lip and just do as the man says."

"I ain't skeered of no man," Willie growled.

"Never said you were," Sam said. "But I don't think you are a fool either."

Their conversation was interrupted suddenly by Tye arriving and stopping abruptly in front of them.

"Don't either of you look around. Just listen."

"I don't hear a thing," Sam said after a moment.

"That's what I'm talking about. No birds making noise or anything else for that matter.," Tye replied. His head was still but his eyes were searching the terrain in front and to the left and right.

"That's bad?" Sam said questionably.

"When there are no small animals scurrying about and no birds making their calls something is the matter. Let's dismount and give the horses a blow and see if anything develops." Tye dismounted. "Look around without making it look obvious."

"You think it's Apaches?" Sam whispered.

Tye threw one stirrup over the saddle and was making out like he was tightening his saddle girth but his eyes were on the ridge about three hundred yards to their right. He had caught movement out of the corner of his eye a few seconds earlier and was now straining to see what it was.

"More of a feeling than anything else," Tye answered. He dropped the stirrup back down and took out his canteen and raised it to his lips, his eyes still searching the sloped and the ridge to his right. Something had moved and he was getting flustered at not being able to spot what it was.

"I think you are loco Watkins." Willie said. "They ain't nothing out there but cactus and mesquite."

"Get your Henry out of its leather Sam and ride on the ready," Tye said mounting Sandy. "Let's ride."

Chapter Fifteen

They made camp next to a small spring Tye had found, made coffee and put the fire out before dark. The horses were picketed only a few feet from them and were munching the foot high grass that was on the bank of the small stream that flowed from the spring.

Tye squatted on his heels sipping coffee and trying like hell to keep from burning his lips on the tin cup. Sam was sitting with his legs crossed Indian style and Willie sat on his butt with his legs stretched out in front tied together. His hands were still tied, but in the front so he could drink coffee. He watched Tye who was looking into the darkness around them.

"What's the matter Watkins," he said in a sarcastic tone. "Still think the boogie bear is out there?" Tye made no response. Willie waited a minute before speaking again, and rather loudly. "I tell you something Mr. famous Scout I..." he didn't finish as Tye kicked him hard in the shoulder knocking him flat on his back. Tye's Henry barked a forty four slug and caught an Apache in the forehead and exploded out the back of his head. Sam fired and another Apache was driven backward by the force of the slug hitting him in the chest.

Tye fell back grabbing the barrel of the Henry in his left hand and using it to ward off a blow from a tomahawk that was aimed at the back of his head by an Apache behind him. He had the Colt in his hand and didn't even realized he had drawn it and fired point blank into the Apaches belly before the warrior could swing the deadly tomahawk again. Tye pulled the trigger again and a red hole appeared just about where the apache's heart was. The warrior went down without a sound. Willie screamed and Tye whirled around to face yet another warrior who was in the act of bringing a knife down to drive it into Willie's chest. Tye fired and the bullet hit the man in the shoulder causing him to drop the knife and spinning him around. A bullet smashed into the side of his head from Sam's Colt.

"Behind you Sam" Tye shouted, but it was too late. Sam jerked his head and the sudden movement saved him from getting his brains splattered. As it was, he was knocked unconscious by a glancing blow from the club. Tye thumbed the hammer back and fired quickly at the Apache and missed. Before he could fire again the warrior was on him slashing at his head with the club. Tye threw his left arm up and took a painful blow on the forearm just below the elbow which numbed his arm rendering it useless.

The next swing by the Apache caught his Colt and knocked it out of his hand. Tye drew back his right foot and kicked the Apache in the left knee. The warrior yelled, staggered back a couple of steps but didn't go down. Tye was quickly on his feet, his Bowie in his right hand. His left arm was paining him something terrible, but some feeling had begun to return. At least he could lift it to help keep his balance as the two wounded warriors circled each other waiting on an opening.

Tye studied the man in front of him. He was big for an Apache, probably six foot and wide shoulders with a deep chest. He wore only a breechclout, knee high moccasins and a dirty, red bandana around his head.

"Kill him Watkins," Willie shouted who desperately wanted Tye to win this fight. "Kill him." He knew what would happen to him if the Apache won and it wasn't a pleasant thought.

The sound of Willies voice caused the Apache to avert his eye just for a second, but that second was all Tye needed. He stepped quickly forward and thrust the knife into the man's belly to the hilt. He twisted the knife and ripped it upwards. The razor sharp edge cut through flesh and organs, gutting the man like one would a deer. The warrior gasped, dropped the club and leaned toward Tye, placing his hands on Tye's shoulders his face only inches from Tye's. Their eyes locked for a couple of seconds and then the man fell to the ground.

Tye looked quickly around for any other warriors, but saw none. He hurried over to Sam and was grateful to see his friend had regained consciousness and sat there holding his head in his hands.

"Easy there pard," Tye said kneeling beside Sam. "Let me take a look at that wound of yours." Sam took his hand away from his bleeding skull. Tye saw it wasn't near as serious as he first thought. He squatted in front of Sam. "Looks like your gonna have a serious headache for awhile, but that's nothing compared to how it could have been if you hadn't moved your head just a instant before the club struck. "Course," he chuckled, "It helped to have a thick skull like you do."

Sam smiled or at least tried to with his head pounding the way it did. "I never knew he was there till you yelled. Thanks, Tye."

"That's what friend's do-look out for each other," Tye said patting his friend on the shoulder. "I'll wrap that head of yours up and then I'll help you and Willie on your horses and we'll get the hell out of here before any of their friends come looking for them." He walked to

Sam's horse and took a shirt out of one of the saddle bags. Using his knife, he cut it into strips and put all of them back in the bag except two. He soaked one in water from his canteen and cleaned the wound with Sam flinching every time he touched him. "Quit being such a namby-pamby and hold still."

"Dammit, it hurts like hell," Sam said growling through gritted teeth.

"A half inch is all that separated you from a headache or being dead, so quit your bellyaching." The wound had just about stopped bleeding so Tye wrapped his head with the other strip. "Just sit there while I get things together."

Tye helped Willie up and on to his horse retying his feet and his hands to the saddle horn. He walked over to Sam. "Ready to try and stand up."

Sam stood up and then staggered. Tye caught him and kept him from falling.

"Damn," Sam said. "Everything is spinning."

Tye held him up. "It'll go away in a minute. Just stand here and be still."

A minute later Sam felt better and Tye helped him on to his horse and then he mounted Sandy. He sat there for a moment cleaning his pistol he had picked up out of the dirt and put fresh cartridges in. He checked his Henry and dropped it into the saddle leather. He looked back at Sam. "If you feel sick just say something and we'll stop." He clucked and nudged Sandy with the heel of his boot and they moved away from camp and into the darkness.

"Thanks for killing that son-of-a-bitch that was fixin' to put that blade in me," Willie said, sincerity showing in his tone of voice.

"Wouldn't want to rob the hangman of the pleasure of hanging you would we now," Tye said without looking back.

Willie didn't say anything for a moment. He was thinking. *That damn man is something else. He kilt four apaches faster than a man could spit. Maybe he is all the things those men in Brackett and Sam said he was. He's found water twice and somehow he knew those Apaches were following us.* He stared at Tye's back and shook his head. *I don't know how, but I will find a way to escape. I've got to."*

"Always heard Injuns didn't like fighting at night," he said to Tye.

"They don't usually. Apaches and other tribes believe if they are killed at night they will wander in the hereafter in darkness forever. There's one thing I've learned about the Apache over the years and that is to never expect them to do what you expect them to do. They are totally unpredictable. Those back there figured they had the advantage of the cover of darkness and killing us would be easy without much risk to them."

"Apaches believe in life after death-heaven and hell and stuff like that?"

"Sure they do. Maybe not in the same way we do. They have a lot of different Gods but the Apache believe in one supreme God, Yusan. Yusan was the creator of all things. They have lesser Gods they worship but Yusan is over all. They believe you go to the hereafter the way you leave. That's why a warrior who dies is buried with his shield and weapons so he can defend himself from his enemies. I've heard some tribes even kill the man's horse and bury it with him so he won't be afoot."

Tye reined up and looked back at Sam. Sam was staying in the saddle but his shoulders were slumped and his chin was on his chest. He looked at the stars and figured it was just past midnight. Where they were was a good spot to spend the rest of the night and maybe Sam would be a little more chipper in the morning. He helped Sam down from the saddle and sat him against a boulder. He unsaddled Sam's horse and threw the saddle on the ground and spread Sam's bed roll beside it. Sam lay down carefully using the saddle as a pillow. Tye put the blanket over him and turned his attention to Willie, untying the ropes and letting him stretch his legs some. His hands stayed tied.

Tye unsaddled Willie's mount and then Sandy. He then went about setting up camp. He gathered some rocks and made a small circle to build a fire to make coffee. He had Willie sit down with his legs stretched out and tied his feet together. In a few minutes the water was boiling and Tye dropped in the coffee grounds.

Like Tye had said before the only thing that gets a man's attention quicker than the aroma of fresh coffee is a bunch of screaming Apaches charging you. Tye saw Sam's head come up at the first whiff and smiled. *He might just live yet*, he thought. Tye filled Sam's cup and took it to him. Sam took a little sip and shook his head, then wish he hadn't. His head told him immediately that he'd better go easy and no sudden movements.

"Good Coffee, Tye," Sam said between sips.

"I wouldn't know," Willie said, "Since I don't have any." Tye poured the man a cup.

"Thanks."

They sat there for five or so minutes with no one saying anything. Each man just enjoying one of the little pleasures a man has on the trail-good, strong coffee.

Tye stood up. "We'd better get a little shuteye. We'll be on the trail at first light."

"What about someone watching," Willie said. "Don't you think we need a sentry?"

"Sandy will let me know if anything or anyone gets near," Tye said. "Now, quit your jawing and get some sleep."

Chapter Sixteen

Sept. 3rd, 1874

Noon on the second day after their fight with the Apaches found the three men crossing the Rio Grande into Texas. Sam's head had quit pounding with every step of his horse and after the tension of the last two or three days things were looking up for them, except for Willie. All he could think about was getting away from these two and escaping the noose.

"I had me some doubts we would see Texas again," Sam said. "It's damn good to be home."

"Amen to that," Tye said. "One more night on the trail and its home cooking." Then he thought of Buff and he wondered if he was alive or dead. Not knowing put a damper on his emotions about being back. It scared him to think of Buff being gone. He loved the man and really depended on him to watch out for his family when he was gone. *That's what got him hurt-or killed,* Tye thought. *Watching out for Rebecca. He always told me he'd die protecting them. I just never thought it would actually come to him doing just that. In a way, as much as he wanted to see Rebecca and the kids, he dreaded going there and finding out about Buff. The thought of Buff being gone scared the hell out of him. I wonder if...*he never finished his thought as Sam's voice from behind him broke his thoughts.

He looked back at Sam just as Sam pointed behind them and to the right with his Henry. "We've got trouble Tye...big trouble." Tye looked where Sam pointed and saw fifteen to twenty Apaches walking their ponies.

Tye looked to the left and on the ridge saw ten or so more warriors walking their ponies. Tye shucked his

Bowie from the sheath in the top of his right boot and slashed the ropes holding Willies hand to the saddle horn. He kicked Sandy into a trot with the others following. He glanced over his shoulder and saw the Apaches keeping pace. They were about two hundred yards away. He nudged Sandy into a gallop and glancing over his shoulder he saw the Apaches on both sides coming at a full run. Willie was beside Tye and Sam right behind.

Willie glaced over his shoulder and then at Tye, his expression showing near panic.

What the hell we gonna do?" He said shouting so he could be heard over the drumming of the horse's hooves and the screams of the Apaches.

"We're going to stay calm for now and look for a place to hole up," Tye shouted back. As they raced their horses Tye's eyes were searching for just such a place. He knew that under normal circumstances his and the other horses could out distance the grass fed Indian ponies, but with being on the trail for almost a week and no grain, he didn't thinks their mounts were in any shape for a long run. A mile went by and he could see Willie's and Sam's mounts begin to struggle. Sandy was fine now, but he knew the big horse would be tiring soon. It was at that moment he spotted what he had been looking for and he pointed with his Henry and shouted.

"There," and reined Sandy off the trail and toward the gulley. He had been over this area many times and remembered the wash. It was thirty feet or so wide and deep enough to protect the horses. They raced along the edge for a minute and then found a way down to the bottom. The wash came down from the side of the canyon and then ran parallel to it. The slope of the hill was steep enough that horses could not come down it without chancing broke legs. There was a huge oak tree on the slope side of the wash that Tye had camped under before and that's where he reined up and dismounted. He cut the rope holding Willies feet and the outlaw jumped down and scrambled over to the edge and looked over. The Apaches sat on their ponies about a hundred yards away watching them.

Tye glanced around taking in the lay of the land around them. He wasn't happy about the circumstances they were in, but pleased at what he saw. Sam scooted in beside him.

"Did you know about this place?"

"Camped here a few times. No water but that oak gives some good shade during the heat of the day plus if you will notice, it will prevent any accurate fire from the ridge up there. The slope is too steep for an all out charge except on foot and even at that, the footing would be slippery with all the small, loose rocks. We have a good field of fire on both sides." He looked down the gully and then up the other way. "The only weakness I see is if they get in the wash and come at us from both directions at once. We have to get some protection for that. He looked up at Willie. "What are they doing now?"

"Sitting there palavering it looks like."

"If they move this way you holler." He looked at Sam. "Can you do some digging and lifting?" Sam nodded." Then," Tye said. "Let's get to piling up some rocks and dirt to give us something to get behind if they come down the wash. Ten minutes of hard, frantic work and both men were exhausted, but they had enough rocks and dirt to get behind if worse came to worse. Tye, knowing Apaches, knew they would figure that out sooner or later. He walked to the horses and got their canteens and extra ammunition. All their handguns and rifles were forty four calibers which made it handy in not having to have two or three different calibers. Tye took stock of the shells and figured they had about forty rounds per man. Not enough for a long fight.

"When they come," he said, "I'll give you a Henry, Willie. I figure we have about forty or so rounds per man so don't go wasting bullets. He walked toward the horses and took Sandy's reins and walked him to the other side of where they were and picketed him. The other two horses were left picketed where they were.

"Whatcha do that for?" Willie asked.

"If we are busy fighting up here we won't have time to be looking up and down the wash watching for Apaches coming that way. I figure the horses will let us know. Just glance at them once in awhile and watch where they are looking and watch their ears." He looked at Sam and smiled. "How's the head?'

"Don't hurt none unless I move it," he answered and noticing Tye's smile asked. "How in hell can you be smiling at a time like this when we're fixing to have us a bunch of Apaches bucks up our ass at any moment."

"You want to know how I've stayed alive out here all these years with every Apache wanting my hair." He paused for a couple of seconds. "I stay calm no matter what the circumstances. If a man panics he can't think straight and it will get him killed every time. So when things are looking bad, I try to relax and think."

"Makes sense," Sam said then added, "I guess," and smiled at Tye.

"Looks like they are getting ready to do something, Watkins," Willie said. Tye and Sam scrambled to the top of the wash and scooted in beside Willie. Tye handed Willie the Henry. When Willie took it Tye held on to it for a long few seconds. "If that barrel starts to swing any direction except at those Apaches I'll shoot you myself. Is that clear?" Willie nodded. "You hear that Sam?"

"Got it Tye," Sam said nodding his head.

"This is probably what they will do," Tye said. "They will divide up and one group will come at us from the left, one from the right and the main bunch down the middle. We need to spread out so all their fire is not coming to one spot. I'll take the middle, Willie you the right and Sam the left. Shoot center and don't waste bullets." The three spread out about ten feet or so apart.

Willie looked at Tye and shook his head. The Apaches were doing exactly what Tye said they would, split into three groups. He worked the lever and a forty four cartridge slid into the firing chamber.

"Here they come," Tye shouted.

Chapter Seventeen

Tye stroked the trigger on his Henry as soon as he shouted the warning and the slug tore into a warrior even as his pony took the first step toward the white eyes. Sam and Willie both knocked Apaches off their ponies with their first shots also, but the rest came on. Bullets whizzed by the three men, but all three held their ground and fired methodically with deadly accuracy.

Tye had knocked three down when the charge broke and the remaining warriors reined their mounts around and fled back to where they came from. Tye saw two limp bodies on his right that Willie had shot and two more to his left that Sam had taken care of.

"We whipped them," Willie shouted, "By God we whipped them," he added standing up and shaking his fist at the warriors who had stopped and turned around looking at where the three men were.

Tye grabbed him and pulled him down just as several bullets split the air where Willie had been an instant before.

"Stay down you idiot," Tye shouted. "It ain't over by a long shot." He looked over at Sam. "You okay?"

"Yeah," Sam said. "I'm as fine as cream gravy." Tye chuckled at another of those remarks that came from his friends lips. Truth be known, all the damn noise of screaming Apaches, thunder of a hundred or more hooves striking the ground, and all the shooting had set Sam's head pounding something fierce again.

"You think they ain't had enough?" Willie asked.

Tye shook his head. "See those warriors lying out there on the ground. They are going to be more determined than ever now to kill us. They also know we are not, as we would say, dumb pilgrims so they won't try an all out charge again. In fact," Tye added looking up at the position of the sun, "They may not try anything else today since it will be dusk pretty soon. "I will tell you this much, I guarantee it will be a long night." He slid down the slope to the bottom of the wash. "You two keep your eyes open."

"Whatcha gonna do, Tye," Sam asked.

"Going to make a fire and some coffee. Like I said it's going to be a long night."

Willie said his voice showing surprise. "You going to make a fire."

Tye laughed. "Don't you think they know where we are?"

"Oh," Willie answered and all three laughed at the remark. It would be the last time any of them laughed, at least for awhile.

A few minutes later the aroma of fresh coffee filled the wash. "Ya'll fill your cups and enjoy this here coffee. Like I said, it's gonna be a long night." Tye was glad they had filled all their canteens at the last spring they were at otherwise they would be drinking water instead of coffee. Coffee had a way of making things right. As a scout on many patrols, Tye had seen it countless times. No matter how tired, no matter how much trouble a trooper found himself in, the smell and taste of strong coffee always had the same effect-soothing and relaxing. It was no different here.

"What do you think them savages will do next, Tye? Willie asked.

"Depends on who's leading them. If it's some young buck trying to make a name for his self there's no telling what he will do. If it's an older, wiser warrior, he will make sure we get no sleep tonight by firing a shot every once in a while and then will attack at first light, probably from where they did earlier and from both sides by charging up the wash. I figure there are still twenty-five or more out there and that would be a problem for a patrol of soldiers never the less three men."

"What do you suggest we do," Sam asked.

"Get the horses in close to us. We're dead ducks if we are set afoot so they may try to steal them. Nothing is more valuable to an Apache than good horses. One of us needs to stay awake while the other two try and get some sleep. We can change every two hours." It was full dark now and no sounds came from the Apache camp or from the white mans. Willie had the first watch and Sam and Tye were lying with their hats over their faces trying to sleep.

Willie strained his eyes and ears trying to see or hear anything that wasn't part of the normal sounds of the night. Tye told him to listen for a few minutes to tune in on the night sounds: the sounds of bird, or the sound of an owl swooping overhead looking for a meal, the horses snorting, moving around on the picket line, the sound of insects and small rodents moving in the night. Any sound other than what he was tuned in to could be an Apache moving in the dark. After a few minutes he was shocked at what he could hear. Sounds he had never bothered to listen to even though he had spent more nights camped on the ground than sleeping in a bed the last few years. He did not even glance at the small fire as Tye had explained about one's eyes taking a few seconds after looking at a fire to adjust back to the darkness and those seconds could get a man killed.

What was that? He thought he heard something that he hadn't heard before. It sounded like it was in front of him. He eased the hammer back on the Henry and listened. He was not even breathing when he heard it again. A scraping sound maybe? A minute went by and he heard nothing. *Had it been my imagination,* he wondered. All of a sudden a figure rose up and hurled himself at Willie. Willie triggered the Henry instinctively and the bullet found its mark somehow and a grunt could be heard and what sounded like a body hitting the ground and then all was quiet.

Tye and Sam were up and at his side in an instant. "What was it?" Tye whispered.

"I did like you said and sorter got tuned in on the normal sounds when I heard something like a scraping sound. I cocked my Henry and then all of a sudden something rose up in front of me and I fired."

"Did you hit whatever it was?" Sam asked.

"I think so. He, or it, was so damn close I couldn't have missed."

Tye leaned forward and with the barrel of his Henry felt around. He instantly hit something with the barrel. Whatever it was didn't move. Tye leaned farther out and grabbed hold of a hand and pulled. The Apache slid into the gully with them.

"He dead?" Sam asked.

"Half his head is blown away," Tye answered, "So I would say he was."He patted the outlaw on the shoulder. "Way to stay alert." A second later, he added. "I think all of us should stay awake for at least another couple hours then we can get a little shuteye.

How in hell a damn man can go to sleep after something like that, Willie wondered, his body still tingling with the excitement of the last minute or so. *I'm wide awake and have no desire to go to sleep and wake up dead.* He thought about what he had just thought about waking up dead-and smiled. He slid down the embankment to fill his tin cup with coffee and then made his way back up and settled in beside Tye.

It was quiet. Since the shot not one sound could be heard except the steady breathing of the men beside him. In fact it was so quiet Willie let his thought's drift back-back to his youth on the farm. There were plenty of pleasant thought to be remembered of him and Lester and his ma. Then there were the bad moments when his pa beat him and Lester unmercifully at times for no good reason other than the bastard was drunk. He missed his mother for a long time after she died. He thought about all the things he and Lester had done-mostly bad things. The only good thing he could think of that they had done was kill their pa. They shot him full of holes as the hate of all the whippings came out. He remembered standing over him and the clinking sound of the hammer falling on empty chambers as he kept pulling the trigger after firing all of the shells. After that killing, it was the outlaw trail he and Lester followed. He could not count the men he had killed and even a woman or two had fell before his and Lester's guns. He hadn't thought about the pain and suffering he had caused to so many till now.

His ma was dead and now Lester was also. He glanced over at Tye. And he's the bastard who killed him, but then another thought came to him. He's also the reason I'm alive. Then another thought hit him like a ton of adobe bricks. He's also the reason I'm going to hang. He was split on what to do. Kill the two men and take his chances on getting away from the Apaches in the dark or stay here and possibly die here or if he was lucky, live to hang. A hell of a choice he thought. Despite his outlaw back ground and the fact his brother was dead because of these two he had actually grown to respect them. If he had men like them riding with him no telling what he could have done. He'd probably been a rich man now and owned lots of land and the women would flock to him craving his attention. He shook his head to rid it of the thoughts like that.

These men were not like him in any way other than they were tough men who did what they had to do to survive. Well, that's what he had done for what seemed his whole life. He hadn't had a choice since he was a teenager and killed his pa. He had enjoyed his reputation and the fact most men feared him. But, what had that gotten him? Sure he had a little money, but he spent most of it gambling, drinking, and poking around with the whores. He had spent only a handful of nights under a roof and in a soft bed the last ten years or so. He had never had a relationship with a woman other than the whores in the saloons. He had no real friends, friends he could depend on, other than his brother. The men who rode with him were loyal only because they feared him, not because they liked him. Any one of them would have turned him in for the reward money if the opportunity came up.

"You okay Willie?" Tye whispered.

"Yeah. Why"

"You just looked like you was a little preoccupied with something."

"No, not really." Willie lied. "Just thinking about my brother and things we'd done, both good and bad."

"I know about some of the bad you two done," Tye said smiling. "What good things have you done?"

Willie shrugged. "Killing my pa was a good thing."

Tye jerked his head around as did Sam. "You killed your pa and you say that was a good thing," his tone showing his astonishment.

"My pa was a mean, vicious man even when he wasn't drinking. He was ten times worse drunk which was most of the time. He'd beat me and Lester for no reason and then beat up ma. We tried to get her to leave him, but she wouldn't. She was a God-fearing woman and didn't believe in divorce. "It wasn't the Christian thing to do," she would tell us. One time he beat her so bad we thought she was dead for sure. He lit out after that and left me and Lester to take care of her. She died about two months later. She never recovered from that beating. I was about twelve or so at the time so Lester and me had to do what we could to eat. Bank took our home so we spent most nights in a small room at the livery where we shoveled horseshit, fed and watered the horses for old man Connors. We did a lot of odd jobs round town besides working at the livery."

"A kid will do about anything to have enough food in his belly. We'd steal things when we could and sell them. When I was seventeen and Lester was fifteen we got caught and went before the Judge Langley. This was the third time we had been before him and he just plum got upset. He said we needed to be taught a lesson and sent us too prison for one year for rehabilitation." He paused and looked off in the darkness.

"The so called rehabilitation didn't work." He looked at Tye and Sam. "Either one of you ever been in prison?" They both shook their heads. "Didn't figure you had. Prison ain't no place for a man and sure as hell no place for two boys. We got beat up every damn day and having to do this and do that for the older men. We got so rehabilitated that the first thing we did when we was released was find pa and kill him and then we killed that damn Judge Langley. After that, it was all downhill now that I look back on it, but for a time we was livin' high on the hog."

Tye thought about what Rebecca had said a few days ago about the young man who had a warrant out for murder. *I bet his father was a brutal man and he just took it so long and then he had his fill and killed him. That was the case here as far as Willie's pa being a vicious man, but his killing wasn't a spontaneous thing.*

The boys tracked him down and killed him. Then they killed the judge who was really trying to help them straightened their lives out. No telling how many men they have killed since in cold blood. Nope, no way you can feel sorry for Willie. He voluntarily took to the outlaw trail and now, he's gonna pay through the nose for being such a hard case.

Sam nudged Tye on the shoulder and motioned with a nod of his head to follow him. They slid down to the bottom of the wash and walked to where the horses stood.

"I don't know about you, but I'm a mite nervous with that hard case holding a rifle," Sam whispered

"He's not going to try anything till the Apache trouble is over with. If we're still alive I'll take his gun immediately and tie him up like before. But right now, we need his gun because the two of us don't have a chance by ourselves. We'll just watch him for the time being. You heard me tell him he's dead if that barrel swings any way except at the Apaches." Tye looked around for a moment before continuing. "You watch for the next two hours then wake me and I'll finish the night."

Sam nodded and crawled back up the slope to where Willie was. "I got it for awhile Willie. Go get some shuteye." Willie slid down the slope to where Tye was and sat down.

Tye stuck out his hand. "Let me have the Henry, Willie."

Willie hesitated looking first up at Tye and then up where Sam was. He noticed Sam's barrel of the Henry wasn't pointed right at him, but close. "What if the Apaches come?"

"I'll give the rifle back to you immediately," Tye answered. Willie handed the gun to him reluctantly and leaned back on the slope pulling his hat over his face. Tye did the same with his rifle and Willies lying across his chest and was immediately asleep.

An hour later, a little after midnight, Tye awoke suddenly. He lay perfectly still, listening. Something had awoken him. He saw Willie lying next to him breathing evenly, apparently asleep. Looking up he saw Sam looking down at him. Sam put his finger to his lips indicating for Tye to be quiet and then pointed to the horses. Sandy was looking down the wash, his ears twitching. As Tye watched another horse raised its head and looked. Tye reached over to Willie and nudged him.

Willie removed his hat from his face and looked at Tye who motioned him to be quiet. He slipped the Henry to Willie and pointed to where the horses were looking. Willie nodded and shifted slightly to get in a better position to fire if he had to. The fire had burned down and only the red glow of coals could be seen. It was quite dark. Willie was sweating profusely and wiped his palms on his pants. Sam glanced every few seconds down the wash, but his main focus was in front of them where the Apaches had come before.

Tye leaned over to Willie and whispered. I'm going to take a look so don't go shooting till you see if it's me or not." Noticing Willie was shaking some. "And try to relax. Take a deep breath or two." He lay the Henry down and pulled his Bowie after checking his Colt to make sure it was good and loose in his holster. He slipped by the horses into the darkness.

Crazy son-of-a-bitch has got some big cojones, I'll say that for him. Man has to be plumb loco to go looking for Apaches in the damn dark, Willie thought to himself.

Tye crouched and listened, straining his ears for any sound. He took another step and listened. Suddenly he froze. He hadn't heard anything, but he had the feeling that someone was very close. He gripped his Bowie tight and tensed his body, ready to spring into action immediately. He didn't know why he had this ability to feel danger, but it has always been part of him and had saved his hide many times. It was a gift from God his pa had told him. Very few men posses it he said and you will need to always heed your feelings, your gut feeling about things because they are usually right.

His gut was telling him now that he was very close to danger. He shifted his feet slightly and waited. One thing a man learns if he fights Apaches long enough is patience. In situations like this he who moves first usually dies. He waited.

Chapter Eighteen

A long five minutes went by and Tye had decided his gut feeling was wrong this time. He just started to move when something moved only three feet from him. He could not see distinctly enough to tell what it was, but he knew it wasn't Sam or Willie. He waited five seconds and when the figure moved again Tye struck with the Bowie and felt it go deep into soft flesh. He ripped it out and stabbed again and this time it sank to the hilt.

The Apache screamed. Tye knew it wasn't because of the pain because Apaches didn't do that. He screamed to warn the others in the wash. Tye quickly shifted the Bowie to his left hand and jerked his Colt and fired down the wash. He wasn't expecting to hit anything but his muzzle flash showed several Apaches in front of him. He fired again and again while backing up to where Willie was. When he reached the horses his Colt was empty and Willie stood beside him firing his Henry several times spacing his shots.

Three quick shots from Sam had Tye and Willie scrambling up to where he was.

"I fired blind the first time to see what the muzzle flash would show. It showed more than I wanted to see. Three damn Apaches were less than ten feet from me. I put lead in two of them and I guess the other ran off.

"Good job Sam," Tye said.

"What did you find back there in the wash?"

"Apaches. One of them and me almost danced we were so close before we saw each other. He was the one that screamed when I stuck the Bowie in his gut. There are two or three down there, but I don't know if they are dead or not." He took his kerchief and wiped his face. "I don't think they will try anything else tonight. They probably think our medicine is stronger than theirs."

"What's this medicine?" Willie asked.

"Apaches," Tye answered, "will select a leader to lead them on raids. If the raid is successful then that leader is believed to have good medicine. On the other hand, if it's a failure and Apaches get killed they will think his medicine is bad and will usually select another warrior to lead them."

"They sure enough hate the white man." Willie muttered.

"The word Apache means enemy. They are taught as youngsters that any one not of their tribe is an enemy and to be treated as such so it's not just the white man. They use to roam a large area north of here, but were driven south by the Comanche and Kiowa by sheer numbers. The Apache has never had the number of warriors the other tribes had plus they never travel in large numbers. A group usually consists of thirty to forty people and maybe only ten or so warriors the rest women and children and the old ones. They do have a special hate for the white man because the white man has killed the buffalo, taken the land from them that their father's father had roamed as free men. A white man's status if determined by how much land or money he has. An Apache's status depends on how many enemy he has killed and horses he has stolen. I feel for them. They live a simple life, a good life and it is being taken from them."

Tye stood up and scrambled down the slope. He stoked the coals and a small flame leaped up. He pulled some dead grass and tied it with a piece of rawhide. He stuck the end in the fire and when it caught and was burning brightly he threw it down the wash where he had been earlier. The flames illuminated the area for a few seconds and showed three Apaches sprawled on the ground.

"Looks like those boys are deader than a piece of old wood," Willie said.

Tye glanced up at the stars and figured it was about four a.m.. He leaned back against the wall of the wash and shut his eyes. *It's been a long time since I was this wore out,* he mused. *I feel like I haven't slept in a damn week.* He opened his eyes. *I figure Sam's the same way plus I'm sure his head feels like it could explode even though he keeps saying its fine. I've been clobbered that way before and I know how it feels.* He raised himself up and crawled up the slope to where Sam sat and slid in beside him.

"Go down and get some shuteye, Sam. I'll watch for awhile."

"I could use some I guarantee you that. In fact, when we get back I'm going to bed and ain't getting up for a week," he chuckled. "Been doing some figuring, Tye. With those you killed in the wash and the two I shot up here and add them to the ones earlier I figure they are down to about fifteen or eighteen men. That's a passel less than they had. Do you figure they might just decide we ain't worth it anymore?

"You'd think so, but like I've said before a hundred times, a man can't always figure out what's in an Apache's head." He looked at his friend. "Now get some damn rest."

Tye lay on his stomach, the Henry resting on the top of the wash his hand close to the lever and trigger. He didn't think they would try anything else tonight, but he hadn't stayed alive all these years by letting his guard down. He glanced down at the horses and though he could barely make them out in the darkness they seemed content. This was the darkest time of the night, a couple of hours before sunrise and the time that Tye always wanted to be on sentry if he was scouting for a patrol in the past or in trouble like now. Trouble always seemed to come at that time –if it was coming.

His head jerked around as a snort came from Sandy. Sandy appeared to be staring down the wash but in the darkness he could not be sure. Tye picked up a small rock and tossed it at Sam hitting the sleeping man in the chest. Sam rolled on his side and looked up at Tye who was pointing toward Sandy and the horses. Sam looked quickly and being much closer than Tye, he could see Sandy and one of the other horses looking down the wash, their ears twitching. Sam nudged Willie and both men slid quietly behind the walls of rock and dirt that Tye and Sam had piled up the day before. The third horse was looking down the wash in the opposite direction so Willie crawled over to the pile on the left. Something or someone or a hell of a lot of someone's was definitely moving own the wash from both directions as all the horses were standing rock still, staring down the draw in both directions, ears twitching.

Tye was certain they were going to be hit hard from three directions as soon as it was light. He slid down from the top and whispered just loud enough for both men to hear.

"First light, they will come in a rush and try to overrun us. Before that time comes make sure you are ready with guns cocked and ready to fire. They will probably be closer than you think so don't get a shock when the first yell comes. I will tell you what I have told troopers when we were fixing to be in a fight for our lives. The men who are the meanest, the most vicious son-of-a-bitches is the ones who will survive. Get my drift?" Both men nodded. "Get your mind set that you are the meanest and hardest man to kill on earth and we might get out of this. Good luck."

Tye quietly crawled back up the slope and waited. *If I had to pick two men to be in a situation with me like this, I could not have picked two better.* He thought and then frowned. *Course I wish one of them wasn't a deranged killer so Sam and I would not have to keep an eye on the enemy plus him.*

The first streaks of grey were appearing and things were barely beginning to be visible when the scream came.

Chapter Nineteen

Daylight Sept. 5th, 1874

Tye was shocked at how close the Apaches were. They rose up from the earth no more than twenty feet in front of him. He knew the skill the Apaches had at becoming part of the landscape and almost impossible to spot, but these warriors surprised even him who had been fighting them for fifteen or more years. He was shocked, but not enough to prevent him from instantly firing his Henry again and again as fast as he could lever a fresh forty-four shell into the chamber. Two warriors were dead before they had moved five feet and another was on the ground gut shot. Another was hurtling his body toward Tye tomahawk raised to strike a fatal blow to the hated white eyes head.

Sam had downed two warriors and was struggling with a third who had jumped him who was now on his back and the Apache on top of him fixing to bash his head in with a tomahawk. Sam had lost his grip on the Henry when the Apache barreled into him like a bull buffalo and he now was trying to prevent the man from bashing his brains out. As the Apache raised his arm to deliver the fatal blow a hole appeared in his forehead and he fell from atop Sam.

Willie now had his hands full as two warriors were charging him and were too close to swing the Henry back around after shooting the warrior that was on Sam. He had killed one when they first charged and wounded one, but now he knew he was fixing to be killed. He steeled himself for the death blow when the Apaches stopped in their tracks. A bugle could be heard and it was pretty close. The Apaches turned and ran back down the wash. Willie, realizing they were gone knew this was his chance, He whirled and fired point blank at

Sam and the force of the slug knocked Sam off his feet onto his back.

The Apache on Tye had fled when the bugle sounded. Tye heard a shot behind him and saw too late Willie's rifle come up at him and saw the muzzle flash and then nothing.

"He's coming around sir," the private said.

Captain McClellan hurried over from where Sam lay to where Tye laid. The private had helped Tye to a sitting position and Tye sat with his head down holding the side of his bandaged head with his hand.

"W...What h...happened," Tye mumbled and then seeing McClellan. "Where did you come from, Captain?"

"Looks like the cavalry saved your butt," Mr. Watkins, he said smiling.

Tye looked around. What about Sam and Willie?"

"Don't know about Willie, but Sam's over there in a bad way. He took a bullet in the left side of his chest. He's hit pretty hard Tye."

"Help me up Captain." Tye, with McClellan's help, stood up and stumbling some, made his way down the slope to where Sam was lying with some soldiers around him. They parted when Tye and McClellan arrived.

"You okay Tye?" one of the soldiers asked.

Tye trying to focus his eyes saw a familiar face and reached out to clasp the man's hand. "Sergeant Absher. Glad to see you."

"Sam's in a bad way, Tye." Absher said. "Keeps saying something about someone named Willie shooting him."

"The bastard shot me too," Tye said.

"You mean the Apaches didn't shoot you!" Arnold said, astonished at what Tye said.

"What happened here?" McClellan asked. "We've rounded up at least a dozen dead Apaches and had to shoot a couple more that were wounded."

"In a minute captain." Tye knelt down beside Sam. "Sam...Sam can you hear me.?"

Sams' eye lids fluttered a couple times then opened. Recognizing Tye, he grasped Tye's arm with his hand. He spoke in a whisper and struggled for words. "The b...bastard s...shot an Apache o...off me that was about to b...bash my head in and then, w...when t...the injuns fled...h...he shot m...me."

"Don't talk any more Sam. Save your strength." He removed Sam's hand from his wrist and then Tye placed his palm on his friend's forehead for a few seconds. He patted him on the shoulder and stood up and told everyone what had happened in the last couple days.

'I sent a dispatch to Clark requesting a ambulance and surgeon to meet us at the Watson's homestead. We should be there by shortly after noon and I figure the doc will be there soon after dark. They can make a hell of lot better time than we can with us hauling Sam on a travois.

Tye, sitting on Sandy, spoke to McClellan. "You get Sam to the Watson's as fast as you can. I know Mrs. Watson and she's a hand at nursing. She can take care of him till the sawbones arrives from the fort." Tye stood up, staggered a little then got his feet under him. "Captain," Tye almost did not want to ask but he had to, "How's Buff." He steeled himself for the answer.

"Last I heard he was going home to Rebecca and them grandkids."

"You mean..."

"Buff is fine Tye, except for the broken arm and some bad bruises."

Tye placed his hands on both shoulders of McClellan and struggled to get the words out. "Thanks McClellan." *Buff was okay, Rebecca and the kids are okay...the whole world is okay.* He looked up as he mounted Sandy. *Thank you Lord for listening.*

"Where do you think you are going?" McClellan queried.

"Tracking a skunk down and kill it."

"You're in no shape to go chasing down a man like that by yourself." He turned in the saddle. "Sergeant Absher," he shouted.

"Yes Sir," Absher said saluting as he rode up.

"Sergeant, pick one man and both of you will go with Mr. Watkins, but if the trail leads into Mexico, you are not to cross the border. Understood?"

"Yes sir," Absher said with a smile as big as Texas across his face. "Will do sir." He started to rein his mount around when Tye grabbed hold of the reins and stopped the horse.

"This is not the army's fight Captain. This is a civil matter."

"I realize that Tye, but the man is a menace to the settlers around here and needs to be brought in...or killed. You're wounded and really in no condition to go by yourself. But the main reason is you are my friend and if you remember, I owe you my career."

"I still don't see wh...." Tye was cut off by McClellan.

"Page 46, paragraph three of military regulations. In certain cases the military may help enforce civilian laws if the situation warrants such help."

Tye looked at him with a perplexed expression. "It says that?"

"Yes it does," McClellan replied. "And this is one of those situations." Tye let go of Absher's reins. Absher smiled knowing that McClellan had just pulled that regulation out of his ass.

"Take care of Sam," Tye said shaking McClellan's hand. "Get a man to cut some big limbs off a mesquite and mash the sap out. Put it on Sam's wound."

"Mesquite sap on a wound?" McClellan said questionly.

"The sap will help hold off infection," Tye said reining Sandy around and took off down the wash following the tracks of Willie's horse.

A minute later Absher rode up beside him with Private Garner.

Tye looked at the man and recognized him and chuckled. "I see you are a private again Garner. Hit another Lieutenant for a stupid order"?

"Not exactly Mr. Watkins. I simply told Thurston what a dumb-ass Lieutenant Schneider was in front of some other men. Thurston dismissed all of them and then listened to my story...my side of things. He laughed, to my surprise, and told me that he knew Schneider was not fit for command and was in the process of getting him transferred elsewhere or at least assigned to a desk job. He added that because there were witnesses to my tirade he could not let me go completely unpunished. So I spent three days in the guardhouse and demoted in rank to private."

"How many times have you been busted...four?" Tye asked.

"Six." Garner answered. "And probably will be more if they promote me again."

"He must be the best damn private in the army," Absher chuckled. "At least he's been one more times than anyone else."

"Sergeant, private, or corporal don't make a damn to me. You're one man I was always glad to see on the patrols I was scouting for," Tye said. "That goes for you to Absher. There a few good men I always like to see in the patrols I scouted for; you two plus, Arnold, Christian, and Phipps." The thought of Christian being dead put a damper on the reunion.

The two troopers dropped behind Tye so he could concentrate on following the tracks of the man they were after. Ten minutes later Tye suddenly reined up and pointed to the east slope of the wash. "He left the wash here," Tye said as he nudged Sandy up the slope of the wash with Absher and Garner right behind him.

Tye was upset at first about McClellan insisting the two troopers go along with him. Sam tagged along and look where he is now. *However, considering the curly wolf I'm after and my condition,* he mused, I *might need them. I've already witnessed the man's shooting ability and with him knowing I'm after him he might just hole up and dry gulch me.* Another thought struck him suddenly. *He shot me. He figures me for dead and no one is chasing him. The patrol would think me and Sam were killed by the Apaches and no one would know about him. That is a good thing.* He suddenly felt better and with not worrying about being dry gulched he nudged Sandy into a gallop. Willie was running his horse pretty hard so the tracks were plain as day besides, the trotting was out of the question with his head feeling the way it did.

The tracks were traveling parallel to the Rio Grande about a mile or so from its bank. The tracks showed Willie's horse was tiring some and had slowed to a trot. Sandy was fine and Tye looked back at the troopers horses. They appeared to be holding up so he continued at a gallop to try and close the gap some more.

Ten minutes later Tye uttered an oath and reined Sandy up.

"What is it," Absher asked an obviously upset Tye.

"The loco bastard is heading toward the river and Mexico."

"That's not surprising is it? Most of the damn outlaws do."

"After what he did a couple days ago over there, every man in uniform will be looking for him."

"They will be looking for a gang, not one man won't they?"

"Maybe...maybe not. If the troopers over there have anyone with them that can read sign even a little bit they will find where we shot it out with them. Cartridges, dried blood on the sand and rocks would pretty well tell the story. And if they did find the bodies which I'm sure they did, some of the men knew what Willie looked like and would not find him among the dead. They'll track us, find the Apaches we killed and then follow our tracks to the Rio Grande." Tye dismounted as did the two men. They loosened the girths on their saddles and each gave the mounts a drink of water poured into their hats. Tye stood with his forearms on the saddle and stared toward Mexico...thinking.

Chapter Twenty

Dawn- September 6th

Tye squatted by the small fire sipping coffee when the first streaks of gray appeared on the horizon. Tye was alone having left Garner and Absher on the banks of the Rio Grande and asking them to find a place close and make camp. If he wasn't back in two days they were to head for Fort Clark.

He followed Willie's tracks to the Rio Grande where the outlaw crossed into Mexico. *I imagine Willie's pretty hungry now since he failed to take any grub in his rush to get away,* Tye thought. Then another thought struck him, one he didn't like at all. *He'll find some home over here, kill the family and take what he needs.* With that thought, he poured the remaining coffee in his cup on the ground, put out the fire, and quickly emptied the coffee pot and rinsed it out before placing everything in his saddle bags. He had saddled Sandy while the coffee was making so he headed out at a brisk pace.

An hour later Tye sat on Sandy and uttered a string of oaths. Ahead was a small house with Willies tracks headed straight for it. Entering the yard, Tye dismounted, girded himself for what he knew he would find and walked through the open door. A Mexican man, maybe forty lay on his back on the floor and hole in his forehead. A heavy set woman was lying beside the bed also shot. Tye looked around and started out the door when he heard a noise that sounded like a whimper. He turned around and searched the room some more. Finding nothing he looked under the bed. A girl of fourteen or so lay there naked as the day she was born. Tye, in his best Mexican spoke softly to her. "Do not be afraid little one. I mean no harm to you. I'm here to help you." Tye didn't know if it was his words or the fact she didn't have much choice, but she reached out with her hand and Tye pulled her from under the bed. She tried to cover herself wither her hands obviously embarrassed at her nakedness. Tye handed her a blanket from the bed and she wrapped herself in it.

Tye gently picked her up and took her outside and sat her on the porch. He told her to stay there. He went back inside and wrapped the man and woman in blankets and went outside and found a shovel. He went back inside the house and filled a glass of water from the pump and took it to the girl. She drank all of it.

"You want more?" Tye asked. She shook her head and wept some more. Tye patted her on the shoulder and picking up the shovel walked to a small grove of willows along the bank of a small stream that ran about thirty yards from the house. He found two other graves there and from the dates showing the man and woman was in their seventies when they died figured it was the girl's grandparents. It took him two hours to dig the graves deep enough to keep the varmints away. Two hours he could have been chasing the bastard that did this, but this was the right thing to do.

He gathered up the man first and carried him to the grave and then the mother. Next, he took the girl by the hand and walked her to the graves. The girl fell to her knees beside her mother's grave and stared into the hole in the ground and began sobbing so hard her whole body was shaking. Tye knelt beside her and put his arm around her shoulders and was surprised when she buried her face in his chest. He stood up slowly pulling her to her feet gently and they stood there for a long moment.

"Do not move a muscle Americano." Tye stiffened at the voice upset with himself that he had been so pre occupied he did not hear anyone come up behind him. He slowly turned around and was surprised to find not one but three Mexicans. One had an old flintlock pointed at him and the other two had pitchforks. The gun was old, but Tye bet it would still blow a hole in his gut so he stood rock still.

"No Manuel," the girl shouted. "He did not do this; he is helping me with momma and papa." Tye saw the barrel lower a little, but not enough to make him comfortable. The girl, speaking so fast in Spanish that Tye could not follow all of it explained what happened. When she was through talking, the man named Manuel lowered the gun and extended his hand to Tye which Tye took.

"I am sorry I acted the way I did without knowing what happened," he said in almost perfect English.

"Don't be," Tye said after shaking the other two men's hands. "I know what it must have looked like."

"Why are you here...in our country?"

"Chasing the man who did this."Tye answered. "This is a bad hombre and has killed a lot of men, even women besides the lady here. He killed a good friend of mine in Texas. There were eight of them. I have killed all of them except him and he's next."

"You are..."he paused, "how you say...an avenging angel."

Tye smiled. "I'm going to avenge my friend's death and these two good people here, but calling me an angle is stretching it a mite."

"Then be on your way and may God go with you my friend."

Tye looked over at the graves and the girl. "What about her?"

"She is my cousin. My friends and me will finish the burial and take her to my home. She can live with us till she is old enough to make her way. We will take care of her papa's place here so it will be in good shape when she decides to come back. There is a small village about five miles up the road. Your 'friend' may be there."

Tye mounted Sandy and tipped his hat to the four and then finding Willie's tracks leading onto the road headed west, farther into Mexico.

Tye sat on Sandy atop a small hill overlooking the village Manuel had spoken of. It was fair sized Tye noted. Larger than he figured and one this size will probably have federal authorities. He would have to watch his step. He nudged Sandy with his heel and proceeded down the hill to he didn't know what.

Tye pulled his hat down low over his eyes as he entered the village. The first thing he saw was a cantina and tied to the hitching rail was the horse Willie was riding.

"Damn," Tye muttered as he saw the sign on the building next to the cantina which was the police headquarters. He sat there pondering what to do. To go in and kill the man was asking for trouble with the Mexican authorities. He didn't figure it would be a wise thing to do to talk to them either. Too many questions could be asked of him and some of the answers could place him in a lot of hot water.

He saw another cantina down the street a ways. He could get a table by the window and watch the street for Willie leaving. That's what he did. He had a beer and a table where he could see the street.

Tye being six two, well built besides extremely good looking brought one of the girls to his table immediately. She placed a hand on his shoulder and leaned down to whisper in his ear. Tye noticed the low cut dress she wore left nothing to the imagination when she leaned forward.

"Maybe later," Tye said hoping that would get rid of the girl. It did after she placed a finger to her lips and then touched Tye's lips with her finger. She was a pretty little filly, but Tye had a much prettier one at home.

He sat there for two hours, two long hours of doing nothing but sipping horse piss, putting off the persistent gal, and watching the street. He had just lifted the mug to his lips when gun shots rang out down the street. Tye went outside with several other patrons to see what was going on only to see Willie flash by on a horse that was running all out. A man in uniform was chasing after him on foot and fired a couple of shots his way but had no chance of hitting Willie who was well out of pistol range.

The officer was next to Tye completely out of breath. "What happened? Tye asked grabbing the exhausted officer by the shoulder.

It was a few seconds before the man could speak. "An Americano like you shot a man in the cantina down the street. When one of my men rushed into the cantina, he shot him too. Both men are dead.

"You speak good English so listen to me," Tye said speaking in a firm voice. "The bastard's name is Willie Mills and I'm after him. He killed several people in Texas including a very good friend of mine. He also killed a family just outside of your village. The young girl is being cared for by a cousin by the name of Manuel.

"I know the family," the officer said. "The young girl is Rosita Morales and her cousin is Manuel Morales. You say they are dead?"

"Tye nodded. " The girl is not, but her parents are. Murdered by the man you were chasing." Tye untied Sandy's reins and jumped on. "I'm gonna kill him."

"The officer shouted after him. "Bring the el bastardo's body to me." Tye looked over his shoulder; nodded and kicked Sandy into a gallop.

Chapter Twenty One

To say Tye was more than little upset with how things were working out would be an understatement. *The man has killed four people and raped a little girl since he got away from me. How many more before he is stopped?* Tye was so angry he had to tell himself to pull in his horns or make a mistake that could cost him his life and if that came about countless innocent people would fall before that son-of-a-bitch's gun.

He reined Sandy to a trot and then a walk as he studied the road for tracks. He had figured out yesterday that the horse Willie rode had a right hind hoof that turned out. Not enough to be a problem for the horse but it gave Tye a definite track to pick out among other tracks. He rode a half mile at a time and then dismounted to study the tracks in the road. If he could not find it then Willie had left the road somewhere between where he was now and the last time he saw the tracks. So far, Willie had stuck to the road.

Three miles ahead Willie watched his back trail from the top of a hill. As he raced through the village he had thought he saw the big sorrel that Watkins rode, but he knew that could not be. He had seen his bullet strike him in the head. *I should have drilled him again to make sure, but damn, I saw his head recoil from the slug. There's not a chance in hell he could be on my trail,* he told himself, but he had lived this long with so many looking for him by being careful and not taking things for granted. *I'm gonna pretend it was him and find me a nice little spot and set up a surprise.* If he had known Tye a little better he would know that Apaches had been trying that for years without success and he sure as hell wasn't no Apache. He spotted a likely looking place and left the road. He dismounted after a few yards and backtracked on foot with a mesquite limb and brushed out his horse's tracks. He remounted and rode into the rocks that were a hundred yards off the road and just the right distance for his Henry.

An hour later Tye sat on Sandy at the exact spot Willie had left the road. He smiled and discreetly let his eyes wander over the terrain, specifically the jumble of boulders about a hundred or so yards off the road. The boulders, some as large as a small house, looked out of place. The land was fairly flat here and then there was a small mountain of gigantic boulders that must have come up from the bowels of the earth eons ago. They were black as the ace of spades like they had been burned.

The marks of the mesquite had caught his eye. For an amateur tracker that old trick of wiping out tracks with a bush might have worked, but not on a seasoned Indian fighter such as Tye. He figured he may be in Willie's sights right now so he quickly threw his left leg over the pommel and dismounted on the right side of Sandy, the side away from the boulders.

Willie had laid his sights of the Henry just about two inches above the pocket on Tye's shirt allowing for a little drop of the forty four slug at this distance. *This is going to be easy,* he thought. He put a little pressure on the trigger and then a little more. "What the hell," he mumbled seeing Watkins dismount on the wrong side of his horse. Now the horse was between him and Tye. Willie eased off the trigger and raised his head just enough to get a better look.

Tye hadn't known for sure Willie was in those boulders so he had slid off Sandy on the side away from them just in case. The move saved his life. With a quick glance over the saddle he spotted Willie just as the outlaw raised his head. In one motion Tye jerked his rifle out of its leather laid it across the saddle and fired two quick shots that splattered rock fragments in Willie's face cutting him in several places.

"Damn," Willie cursed and then followed that word with some more as he slid from behind the boulder and out of sight of Tye. He ran in a crouch making sure he presented no target. He had saw firsthand what a shot the man was. Tye had drawn his rifle from the saddle scabbard faster than the eye could follow and fired two shots, two damn accurate shots, before Willie could duck. He headed to where his horse was tied.

Tye slipped from behind Sandy to behind the stump on the side of the road of what was a huge mesquite at one time. He didn't want to put Sandy at any more risk than necessary. He scanned the boulders from left to right looking for any sign of the man. Five long minutes passed, then ten, and nothing moved. Tye stood up, but was prepared to hit the ground at the first sign of the outlaw. He stood there about thirty seconds before deciding Willie had skedaddled out of the boulders. He took the reins and walked toward the boulders leading Sandy. He held the reins in his left hand and the Henry in his right, cocked and ready to fling a heavy slug at the twitch of a finger.

Reaching the boulders he dropped the reins and went to what he thought was the one Willie had been behind. It was. A fresh stub of a cigarette was lying there along with a bunch of tracks. Tye read the tracks and figured out the direction Willie was moving and followed them around and through the huge boulders. Five minutes later he found where his horse had been tied and followed them till they hit open ground. He jogged back to where he had left Sandy, mounted him and rode about a hundred yards parallel with the mountain of boulders to where they thinned out and cut around behind them to where he had seen the tracks leading away back east, toward Texas.

"Where in tarnation is he going?" Tye mumbled leaning forward in the saddle and rubbing Sandy's neck. Sandy nickered and shook his head. Tye chuckled, "I know, I think he is crazy too." Then added, "Crazy like a fox." Tye followed the tracks, one eye on the ground and one searching for trouble and all the while trying to get inside Willie's head to figure out just what he was thinking. *It didn't make sense him headed back to Texas. Hell, half the lawmen there are looking for him, even some town folk whose family members or friends he has killed. It's just not in his best interest to go there. Then again, it has been my experience that most outlaws aren't the smartest men around.*

Willie had no intention of taking a chance on running into Federales by taking the road back toward Texas. He sure as hell wasn't going to go near the village where he had killed the man and the policeman. His trail led through the hills and around arroyos, but he always ended up going east. They were a half day from the Rio Grande River and Texas when darkness made it impossible to follow the tracks.

Tye thought about not making camp and going farther south and then head east and maybe get ahead of Willie and catch him crossing the river. The only problem with that he figured was at this part of the river there were several places a man could cross unlike farther north where the terrain dictated where it could be forded. Plus he couldn't be sure Willie wasn't going to stop to make camp. He was in a pickle as what he needed to do.

If the man made a cold camp and Tye continued on the current path he might stumble into his camp unexpectedly and get himself shot. If he stayed and made camp himself and Willie didn't it would put him hours behind the outlaw. "Damn," Tye cursed at the situation he was in

It was going to be full dark in a few minutes and Tye had made his decision. With no moon and a thin layer of clouds it was going to be pitch dark and a man would be asking for a broken leg for his horse. He felt like Willie had enough sense to figure that out and would stop for the night. He thought about leaving Sandy and traveling a ways on foot to see if he might get lucky and find his camp. That notion was short lived when he dismounted and damn near stepped on a five foot diamond back rattler while carrying his saddle to a smooth place on the ground. He took a stick and nudged the snake away from where he was bedding down. Hills are probably full of them he figured and all of them will be moving after dark searching for a meal. He didn't hanker none to the idea of getting bit walking around the countryside in the dark so he picketed Sandy, pitched his blankets on the ground and lay down with his canteen and some jerky using his saddle as a pillow. He lay there looking up at the stars and thinking about this man he was chasing.

I've been on the trail of a lot of men the last two years since becoming a marshal and I'll be damned if he's not the only one I cannot figure out just what's going on in his mind. Just about the time I think I know where he's going or what he's fixing to do, he does the opposite. I can't figure out why he turned back toward Texas when the safest thing to do would be to lose himself deep in Mexico. As far as me or the law knows he had no connections there besides the men in his gang. His brother was the only family we know he had. He was so deep in thought he almost jumped out of his skin when a ungodly scream came from somewhere close. It was a scream he had not heard for a long time…a panther or mountain lion as some called them. Sandy's head came up and he nickered and stomped his hooves nervously.

Tye sat up on his blankets and listened, his Henry cocked and lying across his lap. He didn't get a good direction the sound came from and was hoping the big cat would cut loose again so he could. He stood up and walked over to Sandy and rubbed his neck with the palm of his left hand and spoke softly, calming him down some. The Henry stayed cocked and in his right hand. Tye was tense, all his senses alert. He had heard of a few instances of a panther attacking a man, but it was a rare instance and usually was an old or injured panther that could not hunt its normal prey anymore. Sandy had calmed down so Tye walked a ways in the brush and then circled the camp. He saw or heard nothing so he lay back down on his blankets.

~~

At the Watson homestead Sam was resting comfortable, or as comfortable as one could with a hole in him. Doc had arrived and could not say enough good things about the treatments Mrs. Watson had done on Sam's wound. It appeared no infection was coming and besides the pain, which had been lessened some by a generous portion of good whiskey, the patient would be able to travel in two or three days. The Watson's daughter, Melissa, was a pretty little filly of nineteen and insisted on taking care of Sam after the doctor had left the room. Her interest in the handsome man didn't go unnoticed by Mrs. Watson. She didn't object to the attention her daughter showed after all she was never around young men and this man was no drifter. The captain had told her and her husband all about Sam and the fact he was a United States Deputy. Another thing that spoke highly of him was that he was a friend of Tye Watkins who everyone within a hundred miles of Fort Clark knew and trusted.

Sam had noticed Melissa when he was brought into the Watson home even though he was hurting something fierce. He felt like he had been kicked in the belly by a mule when he seen up close how pretty she was. The only gal he seen prettier was Tye's wife and Melissa was a close second. He thought if getting shot was the only way he would have met her then it was worth it.

Melissa had pulled her chair alongside the bed and Sam had been answering questions for almost an hour about things like was he married, or did he have a lady friend and some non important things like his job. He was full of questions about her and her family also and so it went. By the time her mother brought in some soup for the two of them he felt like he had known this girl all his life. When she accidently touched his hand while handing him the spoon it felt like he had been touched by a hot poker. His stomach was doing flip flops and he was sure she could hear his heart pounding. Little did he know Melissa was feeling the same things.

The door opened and Mrs. Watson walked in. "How's the patient doing Melissa?"

Before Melissa could answer, Sam spoke up. “I’m doing fine ma’am. Just fine.”

She nodded. “About bedtime Melissa. Your pallet is made on the floor in front of the fireplace.”

“Wait just a minute,” Sam said. “Is this your bed, Melissa cause ifin it is, I’ll be sleeping on the pallet, not you.” He rose up or started to and a wave of pain shot through his shoulder and he fell back.

“You are in no condition to be moving around young man, “Mrs. Watson said in a stern voice. “You just lie there and get some sleep. In your condition sleep is the best thing for you.”

Melissa stood up. “It’s okay Sam. I can sleep anywhere.” She looked down at him, at the best looking man she ever did see, glanced over her shoulder to make sure her mother had left, bent down and kissed Sam on the forehead, smiled and hurried out the door.

Sam touched the spot with his fingers and thought, *My God, I think I’m in love,* and laughed hard, then winced as the shaking of his shoulders brought a new round of hurt.

~~

When Tye had finally fell asleep he slept soundly, but old habits are hard to break and he awoke well before first light. He put on his hat and shook his boots to make sure no critters had made them a home and slipped them on. He rolled up his blankets and saddled Sandy after giving the horse a few good scratches between the ears.

"Well big boy," he said stepping into the stirrup and settling his butt into the hard leather, "Let's go find Willie so we can go home." The sun was peeking over the rim of the canyon giving just enough light for him to see the tracks.

~~

Three miles up the canyon Willie was up and breaking camp. It was almost dark when he had stopped last night and now he was surprised to see the river which he took to be the Rio Grande only a mile or so away. "Texas," he said rather loudly as his horse looked at him wondering what brought that on. He mounted up and took a good long look at his back trail since he was on high ground and could see a long ways. "I'll be damned!" he cursed. “That bastard just won’t give up,” he said aloud as he watched the rider in the distance following his trail.” He kicked his mount in the flanks and was off at a gallop toward the river the pain in his leg reminding him he needed a doctor before it became infected more than it was. *First order of business is to get rid of Watkins,* he mused. *Ambushing him hasn’t worked before so I need to think of another way.* That way came to him suddenly as he came upon an old man and a small boy. He smiled and nodded to the old man and said in his best Mexican, “Buenos dias, Senor.” The old man took off his sombrero and acknowledged the American. Willie drew his Colt and before the boy or the man could move he shot the old Mexican in the chest. The old man stumbled back a couple of steps and looked at Willie with a look of surprise and shock, mumbled something to the small boy and fell face down on the ground. The boy knelt down and picked up the old man’s hand and held it, looking up at Willie with tears rolling down his face. Willie laughed and nudged his horse toward the river to find a place to hide and wait on the scout to try and comfort the boy.

Chapter Twenty Two

Sept. 7th 1874

On the Texas side of the Rio Grande Sergeant Absher and Private Garner were finishing off the last of the coffee before taking up their post overlooking the river.

"Rumor has it you were a lawmen before you joined this man's cavalry?" Arnold said in a questioning tone.

"Was a deputy for a few years in a few places, last being in Abilene. Enjoyed it, got to bust a few heads and had a little respect from the townsfolk's."

"How come you quit and joined the army at your age?"

"Bad luck. I was handy with a gun…I mean I was damn quick on the draw. Everyone knew it so I never had a problem until some young pup feeling his oats challenged me. I had faced down and killed five or six men in a shoot outs in the past so my reputation as a curly wolf that was quicker than lightning pretty well made men back off when I had to arrest them, but not this kid. He could not have been mor'n seventeen or so years old, but thought himself to be faster than another young gunslinger, John Wesley Hardin who was making a name for himself. He wasn't going to back down despite what I said. He made his play and he wasn't as quick as he thought. I walked up to where he lay, took off my badge and dropped it on his chest. Looking at that kid I knew I'd had enough and walked away."

"Married?"

Garner paused before he answered. He didn't like old memories brought up, especially the ones about his family. Absher saw this in Garner's demeanor and wished he hadn't asked the question and quickly said. "Don't mean to be nosey."

"Yeah, I was married and had two great kids, a boy and a girl," Garner said ignoring Absher's remark. My wife didn't take to my being an officer of the law none too much. We had a lot of arguments about it over the last two years we were together. She said she didn't cotton to the idea of every time I left the house in the morning she wondered if it would be the last time she saw me alive. I tried to tell her that was the way it was out here in Texas that no man knew for certain he wasn't going to be killed every day he got out of bed. She was from back east and never was content at being out here in this 'uncivilized' as she called it, part of the country. One day she had enough and packed the kids up and headed back east. Worst day of my miserable life. I stayed for awhile then when I quit I went back east to join her and the kids. It was okay for awhile but I couldn't handle it Sergeant. I wasn't cut out for a nine to five job and wearing damn city clothes plus it was just too damn boring for a man who had been out here, I felt like I was being choked to death so I left to come back out here."

"If you were a lawman how did you end up in the cavalry?"

"Got me a deputy job in Fort Worth which was a pretty rough town. About a year after I took the job the bank was being robbed and me and the sheriff made a bee line to it to stop it. We did after the damndest gunfight anyone in that town had ever seen but after it was all over, four would be robbers were dead, the sheriff was dead and I had a bullet in my right arm." He paused while finishing the last of his coffee. "The bullet did something to my arm and I could never draw my gun near as quickly as before. I knew if some hot head got his back up and challenged me I was buzzard meat. So I resigned and did odd jobs for a while and then at the tender age of thirty eight, I joined the army looking to lick all the savage Indians by myself," he said chuckling.

Absher laughed. "You and me both, but you know something, the last five years of fighting them I've grown to respect them and their ways. Sure, I know most of their ways are not like ours, but a lot are. The ones I have known that I wasn't fighting and weren't trying to kill me I liked. I enjoyed sitting around and hearing them talk about the old days just like I used to listen to my grandpa talk about his days trapping beaver with Tye's pa and Buff way back then."

Your grandpa trapped with Tye's Pa?"

Absher nodded. "Grandpa was over six foot tall, but you might say he was a mite on the skinny side. Buff told me and Tye that Jim Bridger said he would never be killed by the Blackfoot because there wasn't anything for them to hit," he said chuckling. Ben, Tye's pa, was great at giving out nicknames and since grandpa was tall and skinny Ben started calling him stumpy. The name stuck with him the rest of his life. Those men back then were a lot like the Indians; free to roam the country and do as they damn well pleased when they wanted to do it and had to answer to no one except God above. It had to a great feeling."

Absher stood up and threw the remaining coffee in his cup on the ground, kicked dirt on the small fire and saddled his horse as did Garner. They rode the two hundred or so yards to the river where they split up and found a spot about a half mile apart to sit and watch the river.

Garner had no more sat down when he saw a rider a quarter mile up the river on the Mexican side. He looked left to where Absher should be but could not see him. He quickly mounted his horse and started making his way around thick stands of mesquite and a deep arroyo that he had to go a half mile away from the river to get around. By the time he got to where he figured the man would be he could not see him. He stood in his stirrups to get a better view and spotted the man's horse that looked like it was tied to a mesquite.

Dismounting he approached the horse warily, searching in all directions for its rider. He had no idea what this feller Willie looked like or what horse he was riding. He didn't want to surprise someone and get into a shooing match and it not be Willie. He patted the horse on the neck when he reached him and then carefully made his way to the river. There was a lot of cedar and sage along with the cactus and mesquite so staying out of sight was no problem. It worked the other way also, the man on the horse could not be seen either. It wasn't a pleasant way to spend a beautiful morning.

Taking his hand and pushing some brush aside he could see the river and what he saw made his blood run cold. Tye was almost to midstream. He was three hundred or so yards away, too far to recognize the rider but no one could not spot the horse he was riding, Sandy. Then, there weren't too many men as big as Tye so it had to be him and if it was, the man he saw earlier was Willie. "Damn," he cursed as he realized the man was fixing to dry gulch Tye, but where was he. Tye was a sitting duck in the middle of the river. He stood and ran as fast as he could down the slope to the bank and then ran up stream along the bank toward Tye.

Tye saw him immediately and reined Sandy to the right toward him. The sudden change of direction saved his life. A bullet burned the air where his head had been a second earlier and then the sound of the rifle reached his ears. He laid low on Sandy's neck and raced back to the Mexican side with bullets cutting the air all around him. Reaching the bank he turned down river and raced Sandy along the bank toward where he saw either Absher or Garner waving at him.

Willie was beside himself. "How many lives does that son-of-a-bitch have. I had him dead to rights when he turned. He didn't know why Tye had changed direction till he looked down river and saw the soldier boy waving. He fired two quick shots at him in frustration knowing he was way out of range. He made a beeline for his horse as fast as his legs would carry him.

Garner, seeing Tye was okay started back up the slope when he hit the dirt as two bullets kicked up splattered mud in the air to his left. He lay there a few seconds before he realized the distance had been too great for accurate shooting. He stood up a in a crouch ran back up the slope keeping his eye on the ridge for the shooter. He reached the top only to see the man riding away almost two hundred yards away. He turned and waited on Tye who had crossed the river and was coming up the slope at a gallop.

"You okay Garner?" Tye shouted as he arrived reining Sandy in so hard the big horse was on his haunches sliding and throwing small rocks and dirt into the air trying to stop. Tye was off before the last rock had fell back to the ground.

"That's him riding yonder," Garner said pointing with his carbine to a rider almost a mile away.

"Where's Absher?"

"He was farther down river, but with all the shooting he's probably on his way here."

Tye jumped back on Sandy not bothering with the stirrups. "When he gets here, ya'll follow me." He stated to leave then looked back. "I own you Garner. You saved my hide out there a few minutes ago." He tipped his hat and was off. Garner smiled and started trotting to where he had left his horse. When he got there he saw Sergeant Absher coming in a cloud of dust.

"What was all the shooting about Garner?" he shouted when he arrived. Garner quickly filled him in and both men took out after Tye.

Ahead of Tye Willie was frantically looking for a place to hole up. After more than a week on the trail his horse was just about used up before this run and now he was ready to flounder. He looked over his shoulder and could not see Watkins, but he knew he was coming because he had seen him a few minutes earlier. He looked back where he was going just as his horse went down throwing him hard to the ground knocking the wind out of him. He lay there trying to suck some of the precious stuff into his lungs. He was getting to his feet when he heard hoof beats and whirled around to see Watkins coming fast a hundred yards away. There was no place to go but behind his horse. He jerked the Henry from its leather and scrambled to get behind his mount and lay the rifle over the saddle. Tye reined up seventy yards away.

'That's far enough, Watkins," he shouted. I've got this sight square on your top button so don't even flinch."

"Give it up, Willie. You can't run forever. There's no place you can go that someone won't be trying to capture you or kill you."

"That may be Watkins, but it won't be you," he shouted back and squeezed the trigger.

Tye, at the last word from Willie knew he was going to pull the trigger and dove to his left off Sandy just as Willie triggered the Henry. Tye heard the forty four slug whistle by as he was in mid air. He hit the ground hard and rolled as another slug hit the ground where he landed. He kept rolling as another slug just missed, throwing dirt in his face. He stopped when he rolled into an ancient buffalo wallow that had not completely filled in since its last use many years ago.

Willie knew he had missed with every shot and laid where he was shoving more shells into the rifle and watching the spot where Tye had disappeared. He saw the two blue bellies top the hill and he cut down on them. Both men leapt from their mounts and scrambled for cover which was scarce at the best. Absher lay behind a boulder that was about five feet long but was no more than a foot above the ground, barely high enough for protection if he lay flat. Garner managed to roll behind a mesquite that had a rats den in it. It would not stop a bullet, but Willie couldn't see him either. Willie did the only thing he figured he could do: he shot both horses.

Arnold heard curses from Garner and uttered a few himself. The lowest thing a man could do was shoot another man's horse for no good reason. Willie felt pretty confident in the way things were working out. None of the three could move a damn muscle without him seeing and getting off a shot.

Tye hollered. "Absher, you and Garner okay?"

"Yo," both answered in unison. "What do you want us to do?" Absher asked, speaking just loud enough for Tye to hear but not so that Willie could.

"Give me a minute to sort things out," Tye answered in the same tone. Willie could hear the voices but at seventy or so yards could not make out the words.

Tye knew they were in a heap of trouble since Willie was the only one with a good view and also the horse and saddle he was behind would stop their bullets. Course there was the problem that Willie would have if he stayed with the heat making the dead horse a little ripe in short order. Then he had to smile at a thought that came to him. *The way Willie smelled he might not even notice the horse getting ripe. I know me and Sam made it a point to stay up wind of him when we rode together.* Another thought crossed his mind. *I haven't been out of these clothes in a few days. I probably smell to high heaven too.* He shut his eyes and shook his head. *Get the silly thoughts out damn you. You have a serious problem here and you or your friends could be dead before long if you don't figure something out and quick.*

Different plans of attack came to him but all were dismissed. Suddenly, one came to him that was so crazy it might just work. He called quietly to Absher and Garner. "Absher, do you remember the fight at the springs on the Rio Grande near the cave with all the ancient paintings?"

"Yes sir. I remember."

We had the six Apaches trapped but they were in a better position than we were. Do you remember what we did?"

Absher laughed. "I remember thinking it was the craziest damn plan you ever had in your life, but it worked." There was a pause and then. "Are you thinking…" he was cut off by Tye's voice.

"That's exactly what I'm thinking. If we can keep his head down, we can flank him and get him in a cross fire. Now listen carefully because timing is everything. You two have your single shot Springfield's and I have my fifteen shot Henry. Absher you fire at Willie and you and I will stand up as Garner fires and then he will stand up. I will fire and keep firing as we advance. When I run out of shells Absher you fire, then Garner, then I will use my Colt. As we get close, Garner you move left and I will move right and we'll flank him. We just have to keep his head down and not let him have time to fire. Each of you understand?"

"Yo," from both answered his question.

"When I give the word then." He paused for a couple seconds to let the two get ready.

"Now," he shouted and Absher fired and he and Tye stood up as Garner fired. Tye fired his Henry with every step and when he ran out of shells, Absher and Garner who had reloaded as they advanced fired again. Tye now was close enough to use his Colt with fairly good accuracy and he fired six spaced shots and then they were in position. He quickly fed shells into the Colt and took a quick look at Willie's position. He heard Garner's voice.

"What the hell! Where did he go?" Tye looked could see no one was behind the dead horse. He stood and walked warily toward the horse his Colt held in front and cocked.

"Damn," he cursed loud enough for the two troopers to hear him. There was a shallow ditch behind where Willie had been and he had scooted backwards some time during the fight and high tailed it out of there. Absher and Garner walked up.

"That was a hell of waste of good ammunition," Garner said.

Tye didn't pay any heed to the remark he was down in the ditch looking for tracks. He found where Willie got up off his belly and ran farther down the ditch. Tye looked where the tracks were headed and he didn't like what he saw. Ahead was the biggest and thickest stand of mesquite, cedar and sage he had ever seen. It was like the Good Lord had gathered all the extra bushes he could find and placed them in one spot. But that wasn't the worse of it. Past the stand of mesquite the land was broken, huge boulders lay everywhere and even from where he stood he could see small and large arroyos cutting through the sloping land toward the Rio Grande. It was going to be a nightmare tracking the outlaw through all that plus every step he took he could be in the man's sights. He sat down and reloaded his Henry. "Damn," he said again.

Chapter Twenty Three

Tye stood beside Sandy who Garner had fetched and studied the terrain before him. The best bet he figured was to get around Willie and approach him from behind and try to catch him off guard.

"Sergeant," Tye said. "Here's what we need to do. Willie can't be more than a quarter or so mile ahead of us since he's on foot. I'll take Sandy and ride way to the right of that mess in front of us and then swing north for a mile or so and then back toward the river. That should put me behind the varmint and maybe I can flush him toward you or get lucky and Injun up behind him and catch him off guard." Both men nodded.

"He was smart enough to fetch his canteen with him when he vamoosed," Garner said looking down at the bullet riddled horse.

"Been around him long enough to know this is one smart, vicious hombre you two. Don't go to any lengths to place yourselves in danger by trying to take him alive. If you see him, shoot him. Understand?"

"We understand Tye." Absher said.

"You two spread out, find some cover and keep a sharp eye out so he won't get past either of you." That said he mounted Sandy and rode back the way they had come far enough to be out of sight in case Willie was watching and then he swung east for a mile and then north for at least a mile. When he figured he had gone far enough he reined Sandy toward the river, found some rocks that had a little water from the last time it rained and let Sandy drink his fill before tying him loosely to a mesquite. This was Tye's habit of tying the big horse this way in case something happened to him Sandy could break free and would not die of thirst or hunger. Tye looked at the dangerous terrain before him.

He had taken off his boots and put his Apache moccasins on. He had his Henry in his hand, his Colt on his hip, and the big Bowie stuck in the top of his right moccasin boot. He also had taken his canteen from the saddle and had it draped over his shoulder. Tye took a deep breath, exhaled slowly to relax a little and begin making his way through the broken land back toward his friends. Somewhere in between was a dangerous snake; a two legged one.

Willie had run till he could run no more. He knew he was in bigger trouble than he had ever been in before: no horse, low ammunition, alone, didn't have a clue where he was, and on top of all that, a man after him that was meaner than a curly wolf and one that he could not shake off his trail. He also could not shake the thought that this could be his last trail. *If it is, Watkins and the two soldier boys are going to have to kill me and I'll die hard, taking one or two with me. They'll learn that Willie Mills is a man who will die standing up not graveling on his belly like some yeller belly coward.*

Having caught his breath, he looked behind him to see if he could spot one of the bastards. Seeing nothing he turned and began looking for a place that he could dry gulch the three men from. He knew if he killed Watkins, getting away from the soldiers would be easy if he didn't kill them also. Maybe he then could find a homestead and get a horse and food. If he had to kill the people to get them, well it wouldn't be the first time for that to happen.

He had not traveled more than fifty yards when he spotted what he was looking for; big rocks on the side of a steep hill that was covered in brush. It was twenty feet up to the spot and he struggled a little with loose rocks in getting there. Once situated, he had a good view of his back trail for almost half mile. He smiled as he laid his rifle across a rock and looked down the barrel at the terrain before him. *This is going to be too easy,* he mused.

The land appeared to be fairly flat with only a few small hills, but looks were sometimes deceiving in this country. Tye knew hidden among the mesquite and cedars were numerous small and a few large arroyos that had been cut through the rocky terrain over thousands of years by the runoff of heavy rain. Climbing down and back up some of them and skirting others he kept his main focus on a hill a half mile away. Earlier, when he was still with Absher and Garner, he thought he had glimpsed a brief flash of sunlight reflecting off something and since very few things that weren't man made did that, he was focusing on that particular hill.

"Did you see that flash," Absher said speaking just loud enough for his voice to carry to Garner.

"I seen it," Garner answered." Both squatted watching the hill where the flash had come from. Five minutes passed and seeing nothing more on a signal from Absher, they again began moving toward the hill, but a little more cautious. Both moved from cover to cover in a crouch never moving in a straight line for more than three steps before changing direction. They were a hundred yards from the hill when the air beside Garner's ear was split by a bullet followed by the crack of a Henry. Garner hit the ground.

"You hit?" Absher yelled not worrying about whether or not Willie knew where they were. He obviously did.

“No,” Garner hollered back. “The bastard damn near took my head off though.”

Absher, relieved Garner was okay shouted back. “Stay down for a minute. Don’t do anything till we hear from Tye.

Willie was frantically searching the area for the scout. He cursed himself for not waiting a couple more minutes for the men to get closer so he could have been sure of his mark. The two were not his main concern; where than damn Watkins was had his attention now.

Tye dropped to a knee behind a thick sage at the sound of the Henry. He said a silent prayer hoping his friends were okay. He got his answer when the sound of two distinct rounds fired by Spencer’s reach his ears. *Both men are okay,* he thought, *so let’s get this party over with.*

He started up the backside of the hill working his way left as he climbed. He was again thankful for the Apache moccasins that allowed him to move soundlessly over the loose rocks. When he figured he was high enough to be on the same level with the rocks where he had seen the flash at he stopped climbing and moved farther to the left slowly and carefully testing the footing with each step.

Garner, who was on Absher's right, had a better view of the left side of the hill and saw Tye. He picked up a small rock and threw it at the sergeant. Absher looked at him. With hand motions Garner indicated where Tye was. Absher nodded his understanding. Absher took his revolver out and held it to where Garner could see it and indicated they should start firing at the brush and rocks to give Tye time to move in closer. They did, but at sixty or seventy yards all they were doing was making a lot of noise and hitting the side of the hill in the general area of where the outlaw lay hidden.

Willie was a veteran of many fights and knew what they were doing so rather than ducking his head down while the bullets were busting rocks all around him he kept his head on a swivel looking quickly left and right for Tye sneaking up on him. On a quick look left he spotted the scout and swung his Henry around and feathered the trigger.

Tye saw movement out of the corner of his eye and threw himself backwards. The bullet cut the air where his head had been an instant earlier. Tye fired his Henry three times while lying on his back in the direction where Mills was but his bullets found nothing but rocks. He dug his heels into the rocky ground and scooted back up the slope out of Willie's vision.

With their revolvers empty both soldiers had their Spencer's trained on the spot and when Willie moved toward where Tye was, Garner fired a round that took Willies hat off. The outlaw dropped to the ground and lay on his belly. Garner quickly reloaded and waited for the murdering son-of-a-bitch to move again.

"Damn," Willie muttered in frustration. His plans for an easy kill had turned into a nightmare. Watkins was only a few feet from him to his right and the soldier boys were in front.

"Did you hit him?" Absher shouted.

"Don't think so, but I bet he thinks twice about raising his damn head up again," Garner chuckled.

Absher said. "I think he'll try and get out of that trap he's in so train your sights at the end of the rocks.

He'll have to go right or left so if he tries anything shoot at the first movement you see.

Willie started to turn to make a break for it to his right away from where he saw Tye. He stopped and thought a moment about it and then smiled. *Watkins is smart so I figure he'll go around to the other side since he knows I know he's on my left and figures I would not be so stupid to go that way.* He turned back and scooted on his belly to his left as far as he could without the soldiers seeing him. He gathered his legs under him. *It's now or never he thought.* He jumped as far as he could across the steep slope and heard the whistle of a bullet as it split the air by his head before he heard the report. He stumbled some, got his footing and scrambled around and down the hill as fast as he could run chuckling to himself as he figured he had out foxed Watkins.

Tye had left the side of the hill he had been on, but didn't go to the other side. He knew Willie had to make a break unless he wanted to die where he was of thirst or a bullet so he had waited on the back side of the hill waiting to see which way the outlaw tried to escape. When he heard the rocks and the roar of the Spencer to his left he moved that direction and saw Willie scrambling down the hill. He raised the Henry to his shoulder and put the notch of the sights square between Willies shoulders. The outlaw was forty yards away and moving, but at this distance there was no way Tye could miss. Tye squeezed the trigger slowly and at the last instant, dropped his sights and pulled the trigger the rest of the way. The rifle bucked against his shoulder as the forty four slug was spit from the barrel and toward its target. Willie screamed as the heavy slug tore into him.

Chapter Twenty-Four

Willie lay on the ground screaming in pain. He had lost his grip on the rifle when he hit the ground and rolled the rest of the way down the slope. He grabbed his leg with both hands where the bullet had tore through his flesh blood running between his fingers as he pressed his fingers tighter trying to stem the flow. He heard the shuffling sound of feet coming down the slope behind him and twisted his body to reach for his Colt.

"Don't try it Willie," he heard Watkins voice behind him and froze with his gun only half out of the holster. "Move that gun another inch and I'll blow your damn murdering head off, Tye said through clinched teeth in a tone of voice that Willie clearly understood. Willie moved his hand away from the Colts butt.

Tye reached down and removed the Colt and stuck it under his belt in the back of his pants. "Do something," Willie yelled. "I'm bleeding to death dammit."

"Better than hanging you son-of-a-bitch," Absher said as he and Garner scrambled down the slope where the two men were.

"Hold you rifles on him men and if he twitches shoot him," Tye said as he lay down his Henry on the ground and begin searching Willie for other weapons. He found a knife in a sheath that was in a boot and a folding knife in his pocket. He jerked Willie up roughly to a sitting position.

"You gonna do something about the bleeding from the hole you just put in me?" Willie asked the anger and hate flashing in his eyes.

"Dunno, Willie boy, Tye answered. "What do you boys think?"

"I think we ought to let the bastard just bleed to death," Garner said.

"That would save us a lot of time and trouble," Absher said agreeing with Garner.

"Yeah, it would," Tye said standing up and walking toward where Sandy was tied. "It surely would," he repeated loud enough for the men to hear as he walked away.

"You can't just let me die Watkins."

Garner kneeled down beside the injured man. "Not so pleasant when the boot is on the other foot is it. How do you think all those men and women you shot felt as they were dying from your damn bullets? How do you think their families felt as they buried their husbands and fathers? What about the children you and your bastard brother left by themselves after ya'll kilt their parents? What ab… ." he was interrupted by Tye who had returned.

"That's the reasons we ain't gonna let the man bleed to death," Tye said kneeling down beside Garner. He wrapped a piece of leather around Willies leg just above the wound and tying the ends to a stick. He twisted the stick pulling the rawhide strip tighter and tighter till the flow of blow slowed and then almost stopped. He looked Willie in the eye. "I could have easily shot you in the back, killed you like you have done to so many men, but I didn't Willie and you know why?" Willie didn't answer so Tye continued. "I'm going to enjoy thinking of you in that cell for awhile and knowing you are going to die on a certain date. I can't imagine how that would make a man feel knowing that at a certain time and on a certain day, he was going to die. Have to be a terrible thing Willie to go through that, but you know Willie, you deserve it."

"Aint' it the truth." Absher said chuckling.

They patched up Willie the best they could and Tye made a travois to put him on.

"Looks like we'll be walking a ways men," Tye said as he tied the travois to his saddle on Sandy. Garner started laughing.

"What's so funny," Absher asked.

Both Absher and Tye were looking at Garner. "Just occurred to me what's going to happen if Sandy decides to raise his tail to drop a turd or two? All three men laughed loudly. Willie looked up at the horse's rear end and shut his eyes.

After two hours or so of slow traveling they stopped so Tye could check on Willie. As he did Garner said.

"I guess its true ain't it Tye?"

"What's that?" Tye said as both he and Absher looked at Garner.

Garner chuckled. "That if you want a chance to see action, maybe die, just follow Tye. He attracts Apaches like honey does bees and if it aint Apaches trying to kill him and you, its vicious murdering outlaws trying to.

Tye threw back his head and laughed and then looking at Absher, he pointed to Garner. “That man has my life figured out…and the sad part, it’s the damn truth.” All three men laughed. Willie didn’t think it was so damn funny as he stared up at the horses butt.

Chapter Twenty Five

Tye left Sergeant Absher and Private Garner to backtrack to the Watson's homestead to check on Sam figuring that Willie was in no condition to give them any trouble. When he arrived at the Watsons just before dark he was a welcome guest. He found Sam sitting at the table eating supper. Mrs. Watson brought Tye a plate after he washed some of the trail dust off his face and hands.

"You're looking to be in good shape Sam."

"Looks can be deceiving Tye. I'm still hurting something fierce and weak as a puppy dog." This brought a giggle from the daughter and a smile across the face of Mrs. Watson. Mr. Watson just shook his head and continued eating.

Tye cleared his throat. “Am I missing something here?” Everyone laughed except Mr. Watson confusing Tye even more. He put his fork down and looked at Sam. “What is going on, Sam?”

Mrs. Watson spoke up. “Sam and Melissa have found they have a lot in common Mr. Watkins,” she said winking at him and smiled.

“I don’t understand Mrs. Wats…,” Tye said then stopped and smiled. “Well, I’ll be damned,” he said when the realization of what she said registered. “Excuse my language Ma’am,” he said when he realized the cuss word slipped.

“That’s quite all right Mr. Watkins. These old ears have heard worse, right honey,” she said looking at her husband who had his head down concentrating on the food in his plate. “I said isn’t that right?”

“Yes’um, it is. I’ve been known to let a word slip out every once in a while.” He smiled at Tye. “I guess us men all do at one time or another." He took another bite of some venison and looked again at Tye. "So, how did it go with that man you were after?"

He led us on quite a chase, but we caught up with him early yesterday. I shot him in the leg and he's on his way to Fort Clark to hang."

"You mean you didn't kill him right off?" Sam said surprise showing in his voice.

"Could have easy enough, but got to thinking that sitting in a jail cell waiting to die would be more appropriate than a quick death with a bullet." He looked at Mrs. Watson. "This is some fine vittles Mrs. Watson. Thank you."

"No Tye, it's me and my family and a great number of other families out here that need to be thanking men like you, Sam, and the soldiers for trying to make this a safe place to live. It would be impossible if not for yours and their sacrifices of time, effort," she paused, "and sometimes life. It is us that should be thankful."

“Those are nice words Mrs. Watson,” Tye said acknowledging the sincere tone she had spoken them. “Words that men like Sam and me don’t hear often.”

Mr. Watson spoke up. “It’s true,” looking at Tye and then at Sam. “Men like ya’ll deserve more credit than you receive. I get sick just thinking what could happen to the women out here with the type of some men that roam this part of the country. It’s bad enough now for a man to go to the fields and work and hoping and praying no one comes by and hurts his family while he’s away. I can’t imagine what it would be like it there wasn’t some sort of law out here.” He reached across the table and shook Tye’s hand and nodded toward Sam. “Thanks.”

Tye took the man’s hand and said. “Mrs. Watson I want to thank you. I want to thank you and all the women that come out here with their man. It takes a lot of courage and a special breed of women to have the courage to do it. Most couldn’t. Its women like you that Sam, me, and other men like us do what we do.

Later, the men sitting on the porch while the ladies cleaned up the kitchen, Tye asked Sam. “When do you think you will feel strong enough for the ride to Clark?”

Sam chuckled. "I'd like to say in a week or two, but truth is, probably a couple days. We need to get a report off to San Antonio about the Mills gang."

Tye nodded. "In a couple days then" and then added. "You know it's not that long of a trip back down here to get your wound looked at." Knowing Tye's meaning by the statement they all laughed.

Two days later Tye and Sam left the Watson place and headed toward Fort Clark. Food would be no problem as Melissa had packed enough food for four men. Sam and Melissa had a few minutes off to themselves and Tye saw Sam give the pretty girl a quick peck on the cheek and then laughed as Melissa grabbed Sam behind the head and pulled his face down to hers. She planted a long kiss on his lips.

As they left, Tye tipped his hat to the ladies and looking at Melissa said "Don't you fret any Miss. Melissa because I'll take a strap to this youngun's behind if he doesn't get back down here to see you first chance he gets." He nudged Sandy with his boot and the two men were off to Fort Clark. Tye was thinking of nothing but seeing his two children and holding Rebecca.

They had not traveled more than five miles when the two lawmen reined in their horses and watched a rider come towards them hell bent for leather. A minute later Sam heard Tye utter an oath and then said.

"Bad new coming. That's my scout Dan August and another rider riding like the devil is after them."

Sam stared at the rider headed toward them. "How do you know it's him?"

"Rode with Dan long enough to know how he sits the saddle and that big black horse he's riding. Don 't know who the other is but he's a soldier. Tye nudged Sandy into a trot to meet him and reined in when they did.

"Sho' nuff glad to find you Tye," he said as he came abreast of Tye and shook his hand.

Tye nodded and asked. "What going on Dan? What's the big hurry to find me?"

"Trouble, Tye. Damn big trouble." He took a drink from his canteen before continuing. "Late yesterday, a homesteader in a wagon brought Private Garner in half dead. He had been shot high in the chest just under his left collar bone."

"Doc says he'll live to be probably shot again."

"What about Sergeant Absher?"

"Don't know Tye. Garner was half out of it and was mumbling something about a knife and the prisoner Mills. He managed to tell Thurston about where they were when Willie escaped and the major sent Master Sergeant O'Malley and three men there to see if they could find Absher. He us told where you were and about you going to get Sam so I took a short cut I knew about to get to the Watson homestead to get you."

Tye nodded and for the first time looked at the soldier with Dan and was surprised to see Sergeant Cates. "Good to see you Zeb," he said reaching over and shaking the big man's hand.

Zeb smiled and took Tye's hand. "Good to see you Tye," he replied in that strong southern drawl. Zeb Cates was the uncle of Yancey and Billy Cates. The two brothers who had come to the area around Fort Clark a couple years earlier and killed a lot of people including two unarmed soldiers from Clark. Tye tracked them down along with a patrol and Billy was killed in a shoot out. Yancey was wounded and eventually hung for the crime he had committed. Zeb, hearing of his nephew's demise had come all the way to Texas to kill the scout who had captured them. But after a severe beating from Tye and learning from different people just how sorry pieces of horse dung his nephews had been, he came to terms with Tye. Tye talked him in to joining the army. Cates had wore the grey uniform of a captain in the Confederacy during the War and had now had quickly made Sergeant wearing the blue of the Union Army. ***

"Can you take me to where Absher thought they were when Willie escaped?" Tye asked looking at his scout.

Dan nodded. "That's why I was in such a hurry to get you so we might get there by the time O'Malley does and messes up the area with more tracks. It's only a hour or so from here." He and Zeb dismounted. "Let me and Zeb give our mounts a drink and we'll head there."

***Read book eight of the series-Yahzie, Apache Warrior.

Chapter Twenty Six

A little over an hour later the four men were in the area described by Absher. It only took a few minutes after they spread out for the gun shot from Cates notifying the others he had found the sergeant. When Tye and the others arrived Cates was sitting with Absher's head in his lap giving him a little water.

Tye leaped off Sandy and rushed to his friend's side. "Stabbed in the back Tye," Cates said. "Bleeding has stopped and there's no blood on his lips so it must have missed his lungs somehow."

Tye knelt down beside his friend and placed his hand on his forehead. It was hot. "He's running fever." He stood up. "I'll be back in a moment." He left and walked away.

"Where's he going?" Sam asked Dan.

"You'll see in a few minutes."

A couple minutes later Tye returned with two long pieces of wood. He retrieved a blanket from Sandy and had a travois made and Carter was lying on it with the wound cleaned with little whiskey from Dan's saddle bag and wrapped in a clean bandage made from Tye's spare shirt.

Tye looked down at his friend. "I should have killed that bastard when I had the chance," he said speaking to no one in particular. "His kind never change just like…" he paused remembering Zeb was listening and refrained from saying anything about Yancey and Billy Cates, the sergeants nephews.

"Just like my nephews," Cates said. He noticed Tye's discomfort. "It's okay Tye," he said. "I know what they were and what they did and I'm ashamed for it."

Tye put his hand on the big man's shoulder. "We all have black sheep in the family Zeb. Nothing we or you can do about it or change what they did. We just go ahead and live our lives the best we can and forget the past." He looked at Dan. "Can you get Absher to Clark and the hospital?'

"Yeah, I can but I thought I was going with…" he stopped as everyone heard horses coming.

"Looks like you will get your wish Dan. O'Malley can cart Absher back to the fort and you two can go with me and have a chance to be killed," he said smiling.

"Sounds like my kinda fun," Zeb said.

O'Malley and the soldiers rode up and the old Master Sergeant stepped down from his horse and rubbed his butt with both hands.

"Remind me to get in the saddle a little more often," he said laughing as did the other men. He reached out and shook Tye's hand. "Howdy Tye. Good to see you in one piece."

Tye, shaking his father-in-laws hand asked. "How's Rebecca and the babies."

"Fine," he answered. "Just fine. Rebecca's missing you though."

Tye nodded. "I wish I was with her instead of chasing this piece of horseshit Mills. I need to get after him O'Malley. Can you get Absher there," he nodded to the travois, "to the fort and old sawbones? He's running a fever."

"What happened?"

"We don't know for sure except Willie got a knife from somewhere and stabbed Absher in the back, took his pistol and shot Carter . Just get him back to the fort. I've lost enough friends this last year or so and don't want to lose anymore."

"Let me rest the horse thirty minutes and we'll be on our way back. Privates Bates and Treanor here," he said nodding toward the men, "are to go with you Dan and

Cates. Private Marsh will accompany me back to the fort with Carter and Sam." He looked around the area. "You know where Mills went?"

Tye nodded. "Already got his tracks. He's hurt pretty bad and riding isn't going to help his leg any. We shouldn't have much trouble catching up to him."

"You be careful Tye and bring him in for trial so we can hang'um," O'Malley said.

"Ain't gonna be no hanging Sarge, " Tye said, anger showing in his tone. "I let him live twice now and there won't be a third. I'm going to kill the low life son-of-a-bitch if it's the last thing I do."

O'Malley looked at his son-in-law and saw an expression on his face he had not seen before-one of hate and the look of a man who was on the prod to kill. A shiver ran down his spine and he thought he sure as hell was glad it was Willie Tye was after and not him.

Sam looked at his friend. "Don't forget you're a lawman Tye and bound to hold up the law."

Tye spit on the ground. "I don't have my badge with me Sam and I tried bringing the bastard in alive and look what happened-two more of my friends are hurt and one could die."He shook his head. "I'll kill him, Sam. If you can't live with that then maybe you had better look for another partner. In two years of being a lawman, I've seen a lot of sorry-ass trash that if you give them a break, try to help them; they'll pay you back by slitting your damn throat in a second. Hell, fighting Apaches is easier. At least you know how you stand with them." He looked at Bates and Treanor. "Let's get mounted and get after Willie boy."

Watching Tye and the two soldiers ride off O'Malley turned to Sam. "I've never seen that boy like that."

"He means what he said about killing him. I haven't know him as long as you have but seen enough of what he can do to know that Willie is a dead man. I've been around a lot of lawmen Sargc, but that man yonder is the best I have ever seen at tracking a man down. Hell, he knows what the other fellow, whether he is red or white, is going to do before they know themselves."

O'Malley chuckled. "I could write a book on the things that man has done the last five or six years," then laughed and added. "Hell, no one would believe what I wrote if I did write one." He watched the men riding away for a few more seconds then said. "We'd better get Carter and you to the fort and get some medical attention." They mounted and headed northwest toward Clark. It would take several hours to get there having to walk their mounts with Carter being on the travois.

A minute later they were on their way and O'Malley was reflecting on Tye's change in personality. *I never thought Tye would change the way he has. I was happy for him and*

Rebecca when he decided to quite chasing Apaches and become a marshal, but now, I wonder if it was such a good idea. The boy may be right when he said chasing Apaches was easier. These damn outlaws will say and do anything to get a break and then if you give them one, will kill you without a second thought. At least a man knows an Apache will kill you if he has a chance. This Willie character must be the lowest form of human there is. He fought side by side with Tye and Sam on at least two occasions, ate with them, and then tried to kill both of them and then Carter and

Absher too. He shook his head and mumbled. "He's as bad as Yancey and Billy Cates were."

"You say something?" Sam asked.

O'Malley shook his head. "No, just thinking out loud I guess." *I hope Tye does kill the son-of-a-bitch.* He smiled as that thought crossed his mind and then thought. *Maybe Tye's right. Men like Willie and Yancey has no business being on this earth with decent folks. Everyone is better off without them around and by killing them keeps from having to support them while they are in jail or prison. Killing them is the best thing I guess.*

Chapter Twenty Seven

Willie was struggling with the pain from his wound. Every step his horse took sent a new wave through his body. He knew he was in trouble and like a wounded animal; he was looking for a place to hole up. He didn't know how close or even if someone was on his trail yet, but he had survived this long on the outlaw trail because he didn't take things for granted. If they weren't he knew they would be soon and he was sure it would be Watkins and he had seen how good a tracker the man was. He looked up at the sky and then at the horizons hoping he might see a hint of rain coming that would wash his tracks away, but saw no clouds. He did see a deep overhang on the hill to his left. He knew it would be a struggle for his horse to get him up there, but he had no choice. There was no way he could walk and lead him, not with the way his leg throbbed. It took several minutes and some cursing and whipping his mount, but he got there.

He slid off the saddle and grimaced when his foot hit the ground as pain shot through him. He grabbed the pommel on the saddle and steadied himself for a moment, resting his forehead on the seat of the saddle until the pain eased some. When it did he decided to open up the saddle bag to see if there was anything in it he could use. He found a pan, coffee pot and cup along with a little jerky and coffee. He eased around to the other side of his horse and opened the other bag. He found an undershirt, gloves, a folding knife, and then something he could use; a bottle of whiskey that was almost full. He poured a little water from the canteen in his hat and gave the horse a drink and then put him in the back of the overhang, deep in the shadows. It was a wind-hollowed half cave he had found that was about twenty-five feet wide and not quite that deep. It would be a spot easy to defend.

He had a good view of his back trail from where he was. He took the bottle and sat down, his back against the rock wall and he stretched his wounded leg. He knew it was becoming infected and he would be in trouble if he couldn't get to a doctor soon. He took a good belt of the whiskey and poured some on the hole in his leg. He muffled a scream when the alcohol hit the wound. He squeezed his eyes so tight tears ran from the corners down his unshaven face. When the burning subsided somewhat he tore the clean shirt he had found in the saddle bag into strips and using one of them, wrapped the wound. He leaned his head back against the rock wall, shut his eyes and dozed.

Tye rode with his senses on full alert, half expecting a bullet would come his way anytime from the rocks on the side of the hills they were riding through. Sweat ran down his face and back. The sun was relentless and it's reflection off the white rocks that were everywhere made him squint and reduced his vision. He had his Henry across the pommel of his saddle, his finger on the trigger and his thumb on the hammer. He knew the shape Willie was in and didn't figure he could stay in the saddle long and would hole up.

An hour later Tye was keeling on the ground looking at the tracks and then up the slope at the depression in the cliff. Zeb and the other three soldiers were standing behind him holding the reins of their horses. Tye stood up and put his finger to his lips indicating for them to be quiet and then he pointed to the opening in the cliff about a hundred yards away. *With no shots he must have dozed off or maybe he's passed out from loss of blood,* Tye thought.

He whispered to the men. "Lead your mounts back the way we come for a ways." When they were a hundred yards farther away they stopped in a stand of mesquite. "I think Willie is holed up in that little cave I pointed to. I figure he has gone about as far as he can with his leg the way it is. Since he didn't fire at us I figure he dozed off or maybe passed out from loss of blood. From what I saw of the hill it's going to be hard to root him out." He paused for a couple of seconds while looking back where he figured Willie was then turned back to the men. "Give a little water to your mounts and bring your canteens. Bates, you stay here with the horses and stay alert. Willie's not the only one out here you have to worry about. An Apache would love to get those horses. The rest of us will make our way back to the base of the hill and spread out. Find you a place that offers some protection from Willie's guns and we'll wait and see what happens."

Willie woke with a start and cursed himself for falling asleep. He turned the bottle up and took a healthy swig then looked down the slope just in time to see a soldier slide behind a boulder at the base of the hill. He started to move into a shooting position, but stopped as the pain in the leg was twice as bad as before. He fell back against the rock wall. "Son-of-a-bitch," he cursed. He looked down the slope again. "That's that damn Watkins" he muttered under his breath seeing the lawman to the right of the soldier he saw a moment earlier. He raised his rifle and aimed it at the boulder Tye was had slid behind. As soon as Tye looked over the top he squeezed the trigger and the Henry bucked against his shoulder.

"Damn!" Tye said as he hat flew off his head when the bullet went through the crown. He reached over and picked it up and put it back on his head. He looked at Zeb and smiled. "Well, now we know he's up there."

Zeb could see the hole in the hat and knew Tye had come within an inch or so of having the top of his head blown off and could not believe the man was smiling, almost laughing about it. “What’s the plan now that we know?” he asked.

“We wait,” Tye answered. “I figure that leg is hurting him and it’s gonna get worse if infection sets in which it will if he doesn’t get it looked after. We’ll just wait awhile. No sense in someone getting shot up or killed.” *No one but Willie that is,* he thought to himself. *No way that piece of dung is going to walk away from this and kill another person.*

Two hours passed and no sign of Willie when suddenly the outlaws voice broke the silence.

“I need some doctoring Watkins. Damn hole in my leg is getting pretty red and hurting something fierce.”

“What do you want me to do about it Willie. There’s not a doctor for thirty miles or more.”

“If I toss my guns can I come out without you or the boys in blue blasting my head off?”

“Let me think about it Willie boy. You know you shot my partner and stabbed and shot two of my friends.”

"How long you gonna take to decide?"

"Maybe later today after we heat some beans, biscuits, and make some coffee so we can talk it over on full stomachs."

"Dammitt Watkins!" Willie shouted. "I'm hurting and need some help now."

"You know Willie, with you up there and no where to go and us down here with four guns aimed at you I really don't think you are in a position to demand anything." Tye heard Zeb and Dan both chuckling at that remark. No more talk came from the cave.

Another hour passed and nothing stirred on the side of the hill but a lone jackrabbit and a couple buzzards circling above figuring there was going to be a meal before long. Tye watched them as two more joined in the watch and all four circled lazily in the sky. *Probably licking their beaks,* Tye thought smiling.

"Come on down after you toss those guns Willie and I'll take a look at your leg. Sure don't want you to die of blood poisoning and miss out on your hanging."

Willie knew his time was up. Die here or die at Clark with a broken neck. *Hell,* he thought. *I'm gonna go out standing up.* He downed the last of the whiskey and checked his pistol to make sure it had six rounds. He pulled his wounded leg up and under him so he could stand up. He took a deep breath and exhaled it slowly and jumped up and firing his Colt. "I'll see you in hell Watkins." He shouted.

Tye and the others were caught off guard and took a couple of seconds to react to the sudden change of events. Four rifles roared almost as one and Willie was knocked back against the cliff wall and slowly slid down to a sitting position leaving a streak of blood on the wall. Tye stood up as did the others.

"Don't go rushing up there men. That's one tough hombre holed up there. Let's wait a minute and make sure he's dead." They stood watching for any sign of movement for five minutes. "Lets go." Tye finally said and started up the hill with the men behind him. As he climbed he never took his eyes off the outlaw.

Willie was still alive. He sat propped up against the cliff wall, his rifle lying across his lap. Tye took two quick steps and kicked the rifle away. Willie sat there, his eyes following every move Tye made, but making no effort to move. Tye knelt down beside the outlaw.

"Can you hear me Willie?"

"I hear you," Willie answered, his voice barely above a whisper as he struggled to speak. Bloody foam was running from the corner of his mouth when he spoke. "l..looks like you done kilt me this time."

"Why did you charge four guns like that? You knew what would happen."

"Wasn't going to hang Tye," Willie said gaining a little strength and talking loud enough for the other men to hear. "Hanging ain't no fit way for a man like me to die. I decided to die standing, going out the way I always was…fighting." He grimaced in pain and then smiled. and said in voice that was fading again to a whisper as his strength flowed from him. "Tho…thought you boys were better shots a…and b..be over qu…quick." He died.

Tye looked at Willie's wounds and shook his head. "Told you he was one tough hombre." He pointed to the two holes in the outlaw's stomach and two in the chest. "He should have died almost instantly from those two in his chest.

Zeb brought Willie's horse out from the back of the cave and Dan and Freeman lifted the dead outlaw laying him across the saddle. They tied his feet with a rope and tossed it under the horse and tied the loose end to the man's hands tightening the rope to hold the body on the saddle.

"That's it," Tye said. "Let's go to the fort."

Epilogue

With the case of Willie and his brothers gang closed Tye was enjoying being with Rebecca and being a father to Nicole and Little Ben for the last few days as he waited on new orders from San Antonio. He didn't have to wait long. He watched his partner, Sam, as he walked up the path to where Tye sat on the porch with Buff and Little Ben.

"Looks like Sam has some bad news," Tye said to Buff noticing the expression on Sam's face and the papers in his hand.

“Got orders Tye,” he said as he arrived at the porch. He handed them to Tye. Tye read them, folded them up and looked at his friend and partner. \

“How’s the wound?” Tye asked referring to the wound Sam received when Willie shot him two weeks ago.

“It‘s not going to keep me from going with you on this little trip,” if that’s what you’re asking.

“Where you two going this time?” Buff asked.

“Up north a ways,” Tye said, “to a town called Santa Angela. It’s a town like Brackett here, built close to a fort and is a trade center for the ranchers and homesteaders in the area. It’s a pretty wild town from what I hear, lots of saloons, brothels, and a hell of a lot of rough hombres.”

“What in the world you going up there for?”

“Seems like there has been a series of murders that the local sheriff can’t get a handle on and he’s asked for help. So Sam and me have been ordered to go up there and see if we get a handle on things.”

Rebecca walked out of the house at that time and seeing Sam, stopped. She looked at Tye and saw the papers. “I guess you’ll be leaving again,” she said holding little Nicole tight.

Tye nodded. “First thing in the morning.” He stood up and took Rebecca and Nicole in his arms. “We have tonight,” he whispered in her ear.

They all went inside and sat at the table. “Who are you after this time?” Rebecca asked.

“Don’t know,” Sam replied. “Been some killings up north in a town near Fort Concho called Santa Angela. The local sheriff has asked for help and we’ve been sent to help him.

Buff set a cup in front of Tye and Sam and then poured a shot of whiskey in each as well as a hefty one in his cup. More small talk came from everyone then Sam stood up and excused himself.

“Got some things to do before we leave. See you at the stables at daybreak, Tye.” He shook Buff’s hand and tipped his hat to Rebecca. “Been a pleasure to see you again Rebecca” he said and then left.

Tye stood up. “Guess I’d better my things together too.”

Daybreak found the two lawmen riding north out of Brackett headed to a town neither had ever been too and not knowing what to expect…except trouble and a lot of it.

www.ingramcontent.com/pod-product-compliance
Lightning Source LLC
Chambersburg PA
CBHW030354310726
48979CB00001B/301

9780984473090